D0058403

Whatever After

GOOD as GOLD

Read all the Whatever After books!

#1: Fairest of All

#2: If the Shoe Fits

#3: Sink or Swim

#4: Dream On

#5: Bad Hair Day

#6: Cold as Ice

#7: Beauty Queen

#8: Once Upon a Frog

#9: Genie in a Bottle

#10: Sugar and Spice

#11: Two Peas in a Pod

#12: Seeing Red

#13: Spill the Beans

#14: Good as Gold

Special Edition #1: Abby in Wonderland

Special Edition #2: Abby in Oz

Whatever After

GOOD as GOLD

SARAH MLYNOWSKI

 Scholastic Press/New York

Library of Congress Cataloging-in-Publication Data available

ISBN 978-1-338-62813-5

1 2021

Printed in the U.S.A. 23

First edition, April 2021

for archer wolf maxwell sheinmel
(and courtney sheinmel, his amazing mom)

chapter one

That Did Not Work Out as Planned

Five. Four. Three. Two. One.

Ding!

The timer goes off. Yes! The cupcakes are ready!

"Mom! Dad! The cupcakes are done! Can I take them out of the oven?" I call from the kitchen.

It's 7:30 P.M. and I am making chocolate cupcakes for the fifth-grade bake sale tomorrow. We're raising money to buy books for kids in need. My best friend Frankie is making chocolate chip cookies, my other best friend Robin is making brownies, and my *sometimes* friend Penny is making meringues, which sounds really fancy and also really hard.

"Yes, you can!" my dad calls back from upstairs, where he and my mom are watching the news.

"Carefully!" Mom adds.

I turn off the oven, put on my oven mitts, and oh-so-carefully take out the three trays one by one and set them on the counter.

Oooooh. They smell good. And they look great!

While the cupcakes cool, I'm going to make the icing, and then they'll be perfect. Like, one hundred percent perfect. I'm following a recipe I found online that's called The Perfect Chocolate Cupcake.

I'm stirring all the icing ingredients together when Jonah, my seven-year-old brother, zooms into the kitchen. He immediately tries to stick his finger in the bowl. Prince, our adorable brown-and-white dog, runs in after Jonah and starts begging for scraps.

"Sorry, Prince, no chocolate for you," I say. "Jonah, don't use your fingers. I'll set aside a cupcake for you when it's ready, okay? And are you on your skateboard in the house?"

"Um, no?" Jonah says. He is literally standing on his skateboard, inching back and forth. I roll my eyes.

Jonah is obsessed with his new skateboard. It's blue and white with silver wheels. The high schooler who lives next door gave it to him after getting a new one, and my brother could not be more excited. My parents said he must wear a helmet when he takes it outside, but I guess they didn't specify that he must wear a helmet inside. Because he's obviously not supposed to be *on* the skateboard inside.

I lower my voice. "Jonah, Mom and Dad will not be happy if they catch you riding that in the kitchen. Go outside."

"They said it's too late to go outside."

"Then at least go down to the basement," I say. "And wear your helmet!"

The basement is a good place for Jonah to practice because there isn't much furniture down there. Except for the magic mirror.

Yup. We have a magic mirror in our basement.

For real.

Let me explain. It *looks* like a normal mirror, but a fairy named Maryrose is trapped inside it. And if Jonah and I knock on the mirror three times at midnight, Maryrose sends us into a fairy tale. We've been to thirteen fairy tales, from *Cinderella* to *Hansel and Gretel* to *Jack and the Beanstalk.* I've even been into two books — *The Wonderful Wizard of Oz* and *Alice's Adventures in Wonderland.* We always somehow mess the stories up — sometimes on purpose, but usually by accident. We make sure to find the characters new happy endings, though.

"I'll wear it, I'll wear it," Jonah says. He grabs a spoon from the drawer and scoops up some icing to taste. "Not bad! Missing something, though."

"What?"

He smiles. "Ketchup, maybe?" My brother is also obsessed with ketchup.

"Gross. No. And anyway, it's perfect. I followed the recipe exactly."

"Okay, then," Jonah says. He picks up his skateboard and runs downstairs.

"Be careful!" I call after him. Prince trots out of the kitchen, too, and I turn back to my cupcakes. They've cooled by now. I just have to take them out of the muffin pan and then I can put the icing on.

But when I try to take the first cupcake out, it's *stuck* to the inside of the pan. Hmm. Why did that happen . . . ?

Oh, no. I forgot to put the liners in.

I forgot to put the liners in!

Or to grease the pan. I was supposed to do one or the other!

My stomach sinks. I thought I'd followed the recipe perfectly, but I totally missed that step. What am I going to do? All the cupcakes are stuck! I try to use a knife to get another cupcake out of the pan but that just rips chunks out of the cupcake. This is going from bad to worse.

I glance at the clock above the microwave. It's already eight. The bake sale is tomorrow! I don't have time to make something new. We don't even have any ingredients left! I close my eyes and squeeze my hands into fists. I am not going to be able to bring anything to sell. And I really wanted to help. But I messed up everything.

Clunk, clunk, THUNK!

I open my eyes and frown. That noise came from the basement. What *was* that?

"Jonah?" I call, running out of the kitchen and down

the stairs. In the basement, Jonah is lying on his back and his skateboard is resting against the mirror.

"Are you okay?" I ask him.

"I'm fine," he says, sitting up and rubbing his elbow. At least he's wearing his helmet. "I just fell and my skateboard kind of . . . ran into the mirror."

"Is the *mirror* okay?" I ask. The magic mirror is tall, with a beautiful stone frame carved with fairies. I move the skateboard out of the way and bend down to inspect the glass. It looks fine. Phew.

Oh. Wait. Oh, no. I spot a tiny hairline fracture in the glass.

"There's a crack!" I cry.

"Oops," Jonah says, scrunching his face and kneeling beside me. "Any chance it was there before?"

"I doubt it," I say with a sigh. "Wouldn't we have noticed?"

"We never sit this close to it," he says.

"Maryrose?" I call to the fairy who lives in the mirror. "You there? We're sorry we cracked your mirror! Say you're sorry, Jonah."

"Sorry," Jonah mumbles.

There's no answer.

"Maryrose?" I try again.

Still no answer.

Jonah bites his lip. "Maybe she'll talk to us at midnight," he says. "That's when she answers our knocks."

"True," I say.

I can't help but give my brother a dirty look. I told him to be careful! Why didn't he listen?

"I shouldn't have let you go down to the basement with your skateboard," I say.

"Let me?" he cries. "You *told* me to!"

"Oh. Right." Still. I'm not the one who cracked the mirror. What if Maryrose is mad at us? What if we broke the magic? What if she won't let us back into fairy tales ever again? What if she *can't* let us back into fairy tales ever again?

Did I seriously ruin the cupcakes *and* the mirror in one night?

I take a deep breath.

The cupcakes are definitely ruined. As for the mirror . . . we'll know more at midnight.

* * *

My alarm goes off at 11:50 P.M. and I sneak into Jonah's room. He's snoring. Loudly. I'm surprised he doesn't wake himself. Or Prince, who's sleeping at the foot of his bed.

"Jonah!" I whisper-yell. "Move it!"

Prince wakes up first, and then Jonah bolts out of bed. His curly brown hair is its usual mess. He's wearing a T-shirt, jeans, and green sweatshirt. He even has his sneakers on in bed, which is gross.

"Um, Jonah, why are you all dressed?" I ask. "We're not going into a story tonight. We're just making sure Maryrose is okay."

"But what if she wants to send us somewhere?" he asks. "You never know."

Hmm. Good point.

"Gimme a sec," I say, and race back into my room. Better to be prepared, I guess. If Maryrose wants us to go into a story, we'll go into a story. Maybe visiting a fairy tale will cheer me up after the cupcake disaster tonight. I think of the ruined cupcakes, still sitting on the kitchen counter, and let out a sad sigh.

I dress quickly — white T-shirt, jeans, yellow hoodie,

socks, and sneakers. Plus, I put on my watch, which keeps track of the time at home. Fairy tale time is completely different from the time in Smithville. Sometimes two hours in a fairy tale is an hour at home. Sometimes a *day* in a fairy tale is an hour at home. We never find out until we get there, and my watch is the only way to know how long we have in the fairy tale. Jonah and I have to be in our beds before our parents wake up, and their alarm goes off at 6:45 A.M. They hit snooze once and then get to our rooms by 7:00.

I meet Jonah at the top of the stairs, and we quietly tiptoe to the basement so our parents don't hear us. Our parents don't know about Maryrose and the mirror's magic. Only my nana and Penny (long story) know, and they've been sworn to secrecy.

Prince hurries downstairs beside me and Jonah. He never lets us go into a fairy tale without him.

When we reach the basement, I glance at my watch. We only have a minute until midnight.

I knock on the mirror once to get Maryrose's attention.

"Maryrose?" I call out.

She doesn't answer. Crumbs. Is she mad that we — I mean, Jonah — broke her mirror? I glance down and see that the small crack in the glass is still there. I hope it didn't hurt her.

I knock again. "Maryrose, are you okay?" I ask.

No response.

Jonah rushes up to the mirror and knocks a third time. "Maryrose, I'm really sorry about the crack!" he cries.

Three knocks at midnight. Will the portal open?

The mirror starts hissing! And turning purple. And swirling! Maryrose is sending us into a story! Hurrah!

This must mean she's okay. And not mad at us! Right?

"Let's go!" I exclaim. Prince barks happily.

As we're about to step through, Jonah picks up his skateboard.

"No," I say.

"Why not?" Jonah asks.

"Hasn't it done enough damage?"

"But we might need it!"

"We've never needed a skateboard in a fairy tale before," I say.

"We've never *had* a skateboard before," he says. "And we definitely could have used one."

"But your helmet is upstairs!" I protest.

The mirror hisses again. We have to go this second!

Jonah does *not* put down his skateboard.

The three of us jump right into the mirror.

chapter two

Sled Ride

Thunk!

I land on something hard. And cold.

Snow!

It's winter? I pull up the zipper on my sweatshirt and shiver. I wish I had a jacket on. And a scarf. And a hat.

Jonah gets up, the wind lifting his hair. He is not dressed warmly enough, either. His sweatshirt doesn't even have a hood. He's still holding on to his skateboard, and Prince is standing at his side, tail wagging.

I stand up and realize that we're on a mountain. The very top of a mountain. There is snow everywhere. The morning sky above us is gray and gloomy. There are tall trees all around, and to our left, I think I see a frozen waterfall. Cool!

Ding! Ding! Ding! Ding! Ding! Ding! Ding! Ding!

Where is that sound coming from?

I gaze down the mountain. At the bottom is a town with stone buildings, shops, and cobblestone streets. In the center of the town is a large clock tower. Oh! That must have been the chimes I heard. I think the clock says it's . . . eight? Yes. Eight chimes for eight o'clock. I look down at my watch, which still says midnight.

"Look, Abby!" Jonah says, pointing. "A castle!"

I glance up from my watch. He's right. Beyond the town looms a huge gray stone castle. No surprise. There are usually castles in fairy tales. But which fairy tale are we in *now*?

Then I notice something else. There's a super-long metal fence surrounding the whole town and the castle. The fence seems to be keeping out the mountain that we're on, as well as a forest full of trees and small cottages. A big sign on the fence says:

KINGDOM OF BEBEC. WELCOME TO ALL WHO DESERVE TO LIVE HERE.

I raise an eyebrow. "What does *that* mean?"

"Maybe they only like nice people there," Jonah suggests.

"Maybe."

"And that's good because we're nice," Jonah says.

I guess so? I'm pretty nice. I mean, occasionally I can do mean things, but it's not like the king and queen know about the time I accidentally on purpose spilled water on Penny's art project.

It did not look better wet.

Anyway, I apologized.

"So what do we do now?" I ask.

"I say we go down the mountain and check out the town," Jonah says.

"Okay," I say. "Maybe that will help us figure out what story we're in."

"Haven't we been to all the fairy tales by now?" Jonah asks.

"Not even close," I say. "The Brothers Grimm alone wrote over two hundred fairy tales. Like . . . *The Twelve Dancing Princesses*!" I say. Ooh. Maybe we're in that story. I'm not the best dancer, but it could be fun.

Jonah shivers as the wind blows. "Maybe we're in *The Snow Queen* again."

"We never go into the same fairy tale twice," I say. "Maybe we're in the one, you know, with the spinning wheel."

"*Sleeping Beauty*?" Jonah asks.

"No, we've been to *Sleeping Beauty*," I say. "That's where we got Prince, remember?"

Prince barks.

"Right. But that's the one with the spinning wheel," Jonah says.

"There's another fairy tale with a spinning wheel," I explain, my teeth chattering in the cold. "With the gold? A girl has to spin gold. And a magical guy comes and spins gold for her but she has to guess his name."

"What's his name?"

"I don't remember," I say.

"What's the story called?"

"His name."

"It's called *His Name*?"

"No, I don't remember his name! It's . . . it sounds like Rapunzel."

"But it's not Rapunzel?"

"No."

"Because we've been to *Rapunzel*," Jonah says.

"Oh," I say, remembering. "It's *Rumpelstiltskin*! That's the name of the fairy tale. With the gold."

"So maybe we're in that one," Jonah says. "Anyway, let's go down the mountain and find out." He puts one foot on his skateboard. "Ready?"

Um. Is he kidding? He's not really planning on *skateboarding* down a mountain, right?

"Jonah," I say sternly. "You didn't bring your helmet."

"Oops."

"Right. Sorry, but no. You're not skateboarding down a mountain."

"Oh! Oh! Can we sled down the mountain?" he asks.

"Your skateboard is not a sled," I say.

He smiles. "It sort of is. Just with wheels!"

Just what every sled needs. Wheels.

"Please, please, please?" Jonah begs. "Pretty please with a cherry on top? Pretty please with four wheels on top? It'll be fun!"

"Well . . ." I hesitate. It might be fun. "Okay. But we're going slowly. And being careful."

"Yes!" Jonah exclaims. He flips the skateboard upside down so that the wheels are on top, and sits down in front. "Come on, come on!"

I squeeze in behind him and put Prince on my lap. The wheels are keeping me in place and will hopefully stop me from sliding off. The skateboard slips forward a little. "I'm guessing this thing does not have brakes?"

"You guessed right," Jonah says cheerfully. "Now give a little push with your foot."

I look over the side of the mountain, my heart rate speeding up. I don't know about this. Is it too late to change my mind?

A gust of wind blows into us and we start to slide down the mountain. Officially too late to change my mind. Ahhhh!

"Wheeeee!" Jonah exclaims.

"Stay on this path!" I yell.

As we sail down the mountain, ice pellets land on my head. I think it's snowing. Or hailing? Great. Just what we need.

I hold on to my brother, squishing Prince between us. His floppy ear flies into my face. "Aim toward the town," I say, trying not to get a mouthful of my dog's ear or the hail as I talk.

"Trying to!" Jonah yelps. "I don't have . . . that much . . . control . . ."

No kidding.

We're going faster and faster, the wet snow extra slippery underneath us.

And now we're veering right! Away from the town! We're veering toward the forest!

The skateboard is going faster and faster and faster. We're going like two hundred miles an hour, I am not kidding.

The hail is coming down harder now, pelting us. We have no control over where we're going. No control at all.

Jonah somehow veers us to the left, and we're sailing right toward a lone cottage.

"We're going to crash into the house!" I yell. "Can't you stop it?"

"Noooooo," he cries.

This! Was! A! Terrible! Idea! Why do I ever listen to

my brother? He thinks you should add ketchup to chocolate icing! Obviously, his judgment is impaired!

The house is made out of brown logs and white trim. We're getting way too close to it. In fact, we're seconds away from crashing into the front door!

"Brace yourselves!" Jonah cries to me and Prince.

AHHHHH!

Crunk! We go smashing into the door. I expect us to explode or something, but instead the door flies open.

And we slide to a stop inside a living room.

chapter three

Anyone Home?

"Jonah? Prince? Is everyone okay?" I ask breathlessly.

Prince barks in my arms.

Jonah turns around and smiles. "That. Was. Awesome!"

"That was NOT awesome!" I yell. "We definitely should have been wearing helmets for that!"

Prince barks again in agreement. He's trembling a little in my arms, so I give him a cuddle.

My legs are a bit jelly-ish. I stand up carefully, holding Prince. Jonah hops off the skateboard, too.

"Hello?" I call out, looking around the empty living

room. “Anyone home? Sorry we . . . um, sledded in. I hope we didn’t damage your door!”

I can only imagine how my parents would react if two kids and a dog crashed through our front door without any warning.

No one responds.

“Hello?” I repeat.

Silence.

“I don’t think anyone’s home,” Jonah says.

I take a look at the door to see if we broke it. But I don’t think we did. It looks like we just pushed it open. Wind and hail are now blowing inside the living room.

Maybe this is the kind of town where people don’t lock their doors.

“We should go before someone gets home,” I say.

“Seriously, Abby?” Jonah asks. “Do you see what’s happening out there?”

He has a point. The hail is coming down even harder now, and we’re not remotely dressed for this weather.

At least we’re not all wet. We went so fast, the hail didn’t have a chance to soak us.

"It does look bad," I admit, closing the door so that no more hail can come in.

"Yeah. We have nowhere else to go," Jonah says. "And we're two kids." Prince barks. "And a dog," Jonah adds, leaning forward to scratch Prince's ears. "No one is going to mind us being in here to stay safe."

"I guess . . ." I say. Whoever lives here is probably staying put wherever *they* are right now, too. We'll be really careful and leave as soon as the bad weather stops and it's safe to go.

I take a deep breath and set Prince down on the floor. He immediately starts nosing around the multicolored rug.

Now that I have a chance to get my bearings, I see that the living room is very stylish. There's a big pink sofa with lots of pillows and framed paintings on the walls. The bookshelves hold pottery, like pretty vases and painted bowls. A big brick fireplace takes up almost one wall.

"Something smells really good," Jonah says. He sniffs the air. So does Prince, and his tail wags happily.

I sniff. It *does* smell good. Sweet and earthy and maybe . . . like cinnamon?

Jonah, Prince, and I follow the scent to a big round table by the window. There are three empty chairs around the table, and *on* the table are three purple ceramic bowls with little white stars on the rims. Cute. Each bowl is full of yummy-smelling white mush.

"Oatmeal!" I say. Hmm. Is there a fairy tale about oatmeal?

"Yum," Jonah says. And then he sticks his finger right in one of the bowls.

"Why are you always sticking your finger into bowls?" I ask. "What do you have against spoons? And don't eat that. It could be poisoned."

Jonah's eyes widen and he lifts his finger out of the bowl. "Oops."

I dip my nose close to one of the other bowls. I sniff again. Mmm. I love cinnamon. Even if I once had some trouble spelling the word.

"It doesn't smell poisoned," I say. Not that I know what poisoned oatmeal would smell like. I lean even closer to the bowl and take another deep sniff—

And I feel a little shove on the back of my head. Ahhh! My face is suddenly IN the bowl of warm mush.

What the *what*? I raise my head. My face is covered in oatmeal.

Jonah giggles. "Hah."

"Jonah!" I yell.

"Sorry," he says. But he's still laughing. "It was too easy."

On the wall across from the table is a small mirror. Too small to be a portal home, I think. But I catch a glimpse of my reflection. I have to admit I look pretty ridiculous with oatmeal all over my face. I can't help but laugh, and I lick the side of my mouth.

"It could use a little brown sugar," I say. "But it's pretty good. And it doesn't taste poisoned."

Jonah grins and licks his oatmeal-covered finger.

I take one of the napkins and wipe my face. I hope whoever's house this is won't mind that we've eaten a tiny bit of their oatmeal and used one of their napkins.

But that's all we'll do. Promise.

I glance over at Prince.

Oh, *no*! He has his front paws on the table and his snout in the third bowl.

"No, Prince!" I cry, but our dog has already gobbled up that entire bowl of oatmeal.

I *really* hope whoever lives here won't mind.

Why would they leave their food out anyway? Seems odd. Were they in a hurry to go somewhere?

I notice for the first time that the three chairs around the table are different sizes: One is big, one is medium-sized, and one is small, like for a kid.

Same with the purple bowls. One big (and now empty, thanks to Prince). One medium-sized (with a finger swipe in it, thanks to Jonah). And the third one is small (with a face-sized dent in it, again thanks to Jonah).

And the three spoons. Yup, you guessed it. One big. One medium. And one small.

Three of everything. Different sizes.

That's ringing a bell.

"Hey, Abby, look at that," Jonah says, pointing to one of the framed paintings on the wall. "Do you think they live here?"

I turn to look. It's a nice illustration of a big bear, a medium-sized bear, and a baby bear — a cub — cuddled together and smiling, under the words THE BEAR FAMILY.

Bear family.

Three of everything.

One big. One medium. One small.

I gasp as my eyes widen. That's it!

It's not oatmeal in the bowls — it's porridge! Although maybe porridge and oatmeal are the same thing?

"I know what fairy tale we're in!" I tell Jonah.

chapter four

All about the Bears

"Is it *Peter Pan*?" Jonah asks.

"What? Where did that come from?" I ask. "What about a bear family and three bowls of porridge screams *Peter Pan*?"

"I don't know," Jonah says with a sigh. "Just feeling hopeful. We already went to *Jack and the Beanstalk*, and *Peter Pan* is my next favorite."

"But *Peter Pan* is a book and not a fairy tale," I say. "And the mirror always takes us into fairy tales."

He shrugs. "You never know. So you don't think we're in *Peter Pan*?"

“No. Three chairs. Three bowls . . .”

“*The Three Little Pigs*?” he asks.

“No!” I say, exasperated. “We’re in *Goldilocks and the Three Bears*.”

“Ooooooh! Cool. What’s that story again? Do they blow the house down?”

“No,” I say. “That’s *The Three Little Pigs*.” I take a seat in the medium chair. It’s REALLY soft. “Come sit and I’ll tell you all about it.”

Jonah grins. He squeezes himself into the small chair, even though he barely fits in it. Prince, full of oatmeal — or porridge — has curled up on the floor and is napping.

“Okay,” I say. “*Goldilocks and the Three Bears*. There are a few versions of the story. But I’ll tell the one most people know. So, there was a girl named Goldilocks. And she went for a walk in the woods —”

“She went for a walk in this weather?” Jonah asks.

“Hmm,” I say. “I guess so? Anyway! She saw a cottage. She knocked on the door, but when no one answered, she went inside. But no one was there.”

He shakes his head. “She just went inside? Hello, trespasser!”

"We did the same thing," I say.

"By accident," he reminds me.

"I suppose," I say. "So then she saw the three bowls of porridge on the table. And she tasted the first one. It was too hot. The second was too cold."

"Mine was cold!" Jonah says.

"But the third one, the baby's porridge, was just right," I say. "Mine was warm, so I guess you stuck my face in the baby's porridge."

"I guess," he says. "And Prince got the hot one, but he obviously didn't mind."

Prince snores contentedly.

Jonah looks around the room. "But where are the bears? Why would they just leave their bowls of porridge out?"

"Um . . . one version of the story says that the bears tried their porridge but it was too hot and so they went for a walk while it cooled down. But these bowls of porridge are all different temperatures, so . . . not sure."

"Why do bears even live in a house?" Jonah asks. "Don't bears usually sleep in the woods?"

"Good question," I say. "Maybe the bears aren't real

bears. Maybe they're people. And that painting is just . . . symbolic. Maybe their last name is Bear!"

Jonah's eyes light up. "Yeah! There's a kid with the last name Bear in my class. Ted Bear!"

"His name is Ted Bear?" I ask in shock. "Really? Do you call him Teddy?"

"What? No. Why would I . . ." His mouth drops open. "Teddy Bear! Ahahaha! That's amazing! I wonder if he noticed that."

"I'm sure someone has mentioned it to him before," I say.

He nods. "Perhaps."

"Anyway. Where was I?"

"Wait, should we be sitting here? What if the bears come back? And try to eat us?" Now Jonah looks worried. I feel a little worried, too — the bears in the painting look nice, but actual bears are big and SCARY.

"Well," I say, to calm both myself and my brother, "the weather *is* awful outside, so I can't imagine they're on their way back. Plus, it's not the bears that come home first in the story. Goldilocks does. And she's not even here yet, so we have some time. Don't you want to hear the rest?"

"Yes! Go on!"

"Okay, so after eating the porridge, Goldilocks sees three chairs. She tries the big one. It's too hard. She tries the medium-sized one. It's too soft. She tries the small one. And it's just right. But she's a little too big for it and it breaks into pieces."

Jonah's eyes pop open. He looks down at his chair. "Maybe I should get out of the chair."

"Yeah, don't break the chair," I say. I help my brother stand up super carefully. He goes to sit on his skateboard instead, wheeling a bit from side to side.

"What happens next?" he asks.

"So Goldilocks is feeling tired —"

"From all the eating and sitting?" Jonah laughs.

"And walking," I say, giggling. "She goes into the bedroom and sees three beds. She tries the big bed. It's too hard. She tries the medium-sized one. It's too soft. She tries the small bed and it's —"

"Just right!" Jonah calls out.

"Exactly. So she curls up and goes to sleep."

"And then the bears come home?"

"Yup. The father bear growls and says, 'Someone's been eating my porridge!' And the mother bear says,

'Someone's been eating *my* porridge!' And the baby bear says, 'Someone's been eating *my* porridge — and ate it all up!'"

"Oops," Jonah says. "Didn't Prince eat up one of the porridges?"

I cringe. He did. But hopefully that won't change the story, right? Goldilocks will still eat the baby's porridge when she gets here. If she doesn't mind the imprint of my face.

"Then they see the chairs," I continue, "and the dad says, 'Someone's been sitting in my chair!' The mom bear says the same thing, and then the baby bear also says the same. And adds, 'And broke it!'"

"At least we didn't do that," Jonah says.

"Yay us," I say. "And at least we know we got here before Goldilocks."

Jonah frowns. "How do we know?"

"The chair isn't broken!"

"Right." He motions for me to go on.

"Okay, so then the bears go into the bedroom. The father bear says, 'Someone's been sleeping in my bed.' The mother bear says the same thing. And the baby bear cries and says, 'Someone's been sleeping in my bed . . . and is still there!'"

"Busted," Jonah says.

I laugh. "Totally. The bears growl, and Goldilocks wakes up and sees them. She rushes out of the house and they never see her again. The end."

Jonah looks relieved. "So the bears don't eat Goldilocks?" he asks.

"Not that I know of."

"Can we go see the beds?" Jonah asks.

"Really?"

"I don't want to *sleep* in them, but maybe we can jump on them?"

"I do *not* think that's a good idea," I say. "What if we break them?" I glance out the window. The hail is still coming down, but I'm beginning to think we should get out of here, before Goldilocks or the bears come home. Maybe we can look for shelter somewhere else. "I think we should go, actually."

"But what about the weather?" Jonah asks.

"Still." I shiver. "We ought to leave before we mess

anything else up. Prince! Wake up, Prince! We're leaving." I snap my fingers at him.

Prince wakes up with a start. But instead of coming to me, he bounces up and darts into another room, his brown tail wagging. Prince loves to explore.

"Prince, come back here!" I yell.

He does not listen.

"Prinnnnnnce." I stand up, and Jonah and I follow our dog into the bedroom.

The bedroom!

Oh, wow.

It's just like in the fairy tale. The three beds are lined up next to one another, about a foot apart. Not that much privacy. The one on the left is the biggest. Then there's the medium-sized one. And the last one is small. Each bed is stacked with three lumpy-looking mattresses, one on top of another. Thankfully they're not stacked as high as the mattresses in *The Princess and the Pea*.

Prince jumps up onto the big bed. He even does his usual doggie thing of turning around three times before curling up to take another nap.

“Off,” I command. I point to the floor.

He jumps onto the medium-sized bed instead. I see him sink down a bit in the center.

“Off!” I insist.

He jumps onto the littlest bed. Again, he turns around three times, then curls up and immediately closes his eyes.

“Off!” I say again, but this time he ignores me.

“Come on, Abby,” Jonah says. “I know you want to try the beds. We have to try the beds!”

I glance out into the still-empty living room. We are the only ones here, and probably will be for a while. I guess it couldn’t hurt to try the beds, right? Very quickly. I mean, how often does anyone get to try out the famous beds from *Goldilocks and the Three Bears*?

Not that often.

It would be wrong *not* to try them. A crime, even.

Before I can talk myself out of it, I lie down on the big bed. CRUNCH. Wow, that sound was weird. And this mattress is so hard.

Jonah lies down on the medium-sized one. “Too soft,” he says, jumping up.

I try that one next. It's practically a water bed — I almost sink to the floor. It makes a smaller crunching sound, and I notice a piece of straw sticking out of the side.

Jonah squeezes in beside Prince on the small bed. There's another crunching sound, but not as loud as the first one.

"Now *this* is comfortable," Jonah says, yawning. "It's just right."

I squeeze in beside them to see. This bed is not too hard. Not too soft.

It really is just right.

"We'll leave in a minute," I say, but suddenly I feel drowsy. I could fall asleep here. I mean, it *is* after midnight at home. I take a quick look at my watch. It says 12:12. Beside the bed is an alarm clock. It says 9:00 A.M. I do the math with my finger in the air. So, since we got here at 8:00 A.M., that means . . . every twelve minutes at home is one hour here.

Squeak! Creeeeeeeeak!

I gasp at the sudden noise. Someone's coming in the front door!

"The bears!" I say.

"But you said it would be Goldilocks!" Jonah whisper-shouts.

Right. I *did* say that. "Maybe we should still hide. So we don't mess the story up!"

"'Kay!" Jonah says. He jumps off the bed and hides behind the half-open door.

I prop a pillow up against Prince so he's hidden. Then I crawl under the covers and pull the blanket over myself.

I hear footsteps in the living room. Goldilocks is here!

Goldie

Can you see her?” I whisper to Jonah. I’m under the covers. I don’t know what’s happening!

“I’m looking through the crack in the door,” he says. “I see someone!”

“Is it Goldilocks?” I ask.

“It’s . . . a girl. And she has curly blond hair that goes all the way to her waist. She’s definitely not a bear.”

I was right! I love being right.

“She’s around your age, Abby,” Jonah adds. “She kind of looks like Penny.”

"What's she doing?" I whisper. Should I peek out? Probably not.

I don't know *that* much about Goldilocks except that she breaks into other people's houses and uses their stuff. She might not react nicely to catching us here. On the other hand, we're doing the same thing she is. So maybe she'll really like us. Who knows?

"She's just standing in the living room," Jonah says. "Looking around."

I wonder what she's looking for.

"I think she's cold," he adds. "She's shivering. And she has a ton of little ice balls in her hair. Now she's opening the closet and looking around. Now she's opening drawers in the cabinet."

Hmm. Maybe she's looking for a hair dryer. Or a towel. "And now?"

"She's walking over to the sofa," he says. "She's sticking her hands between the cushions. She's definitely looking for something."

So strange. I don't remember her looking for anything in the fairy tale. She just eats the porridge, breaks the chair, and naps in the bed.

"Now she's walking over to the table," Jonah whispers.

"Is she trying the porridge?" I ask.

"No," Jonah says, watching. "She looked inside each bowl and made a 'that's gross' face."

Oh, yeah. Because of my face dent, Jonah's finger swipe, and Prince's slobbery eating-up of all the porridge. Oops.

"Is she sitting in the chairs?"

"No!" he says. "Maybe without the porridge she's not taking a sitting break?"

I hear footsteps headed to the bedroom. I freeze.

"She's coming this way, Abby!" Jonah whispers.

"Be super quiet," I say.

The door creaks as Goldilocks pushes it open.

I hope Jonah's not getting smushed.

"Maybe I should look under the covers," she says out loud.

Look for what?

I hear her beside the big bed, pulling down the covers. She sighs. Then she yawns. "Nothing here," she says. "Do I have time for a quick nap? I bet I do. They should be gone for a bit. And the beds look warm. Then I can look some more." I hear crunching as she climbs into the big bed. And then, "Way too hard, never mind."

I hear her move to the medium bed. "Nothing here, either. And ugh, too soft!"

Uh-oh. Oh, boy. I know what's next. What do I do, what do I do?

The blanket covering me is pulled back.

"Ahhhhh!" Goldilocks screams.

"Ahhh!" I scream back.

Woof! Prince adds.

I stare at Goldilocks. Jonah is right — she's definitely around my age, maybe a year older. Her golden-blond hair is long and curly and looks like it hasn't been combed in a while. She has big green eyes and pale skin. She's very thin. Her sweater is tattered — there are a few holes in it. Her pants are faded, and the hems are all scruffy. And her boots are scuffed.

"Would you stop screaming?" she asks. "Why are you even here? No one was supposed to be here!"

"Sorry," I say. "We wanted to leave before you came but —"

She frowns. "You knew I was coming?"

"Um . . . I mean, we heard you walk in!" I try to cover.

Goldilocks is still looking at me suspiciously. This close

to her, I can see slight dark circles under her eyes. She looks so tired. I wonder why. What's going on with Goldilocks?

Suddenly, she lets out a big yawn. "That bed looks so comfy and warm." She nods wistfully at the mattress I'm lying on.

"It is," I tell her. "It's not too hard or soft. It's —"

"Just right," Goldilocks finishes, and gives me a small smile.

"Yeah," I say. "Do you want to sit?" I offer, making room for her.

"Just for a moment," she says, and plops down. "Ahhh. Perfect." Then she glances at me. "Who are you, anyway?"

"I'm Abby," I say. "And that boy behind the door is my brother, Jonah."

She jumps, startled. "What boy?"

Jonah steps out from behind the door and gives a little wave.

Prince scurries from under the bed and sniffs the girl's brown boot.

"This is our dog, Prince," I say. "And you must be Goldilocks!"

She looks at me with suspicion again. "Yes. Everyone calls me Goldie. But how did you know my name?"

Squeak! Creeeeeeeak!

Oh, no. The front door is opening again.

That must be the bears.

Maybe they're people. Nice people! Without super-sharp teeth and claws.

"ROAR!"

"ROAR-GROWL!"

They don't sound like people. They sound like . . . bears.

"HIDE!" I shriek. Goldilocks jumps up and hides behind the window curtains. I pull the covers back over my head but peek out through the side so I can see. Jonah runs back behind the door. Prince slides under the father bear's bed. From where I'm lying, I have a clear line of sight through the house. And I see a huge brown furry bear who looks very angry.

"Someone brought a skateboard into our house!" the bear growls.

Uh-oh.

He must be the father bear. He's wearing a button-down shirt with gray pants, and small round glasses. That makes him slightly less scary. Beside him is a medium-sized brown furry bear wearing a purple raincoat with a hood — the mother bear. And she's holding hands with a small bear. The baby bear? She looks more like a kid bear. She's wearing a pink tutu over an orange jumpsuit and a blue cap. She also has on rain boots with frogs on them. I might have had those same rain boots.

"Wow, a skateboard!" the kid bear says. But her parents are already rushing over to look at the table.

"Someone's been eating our porridge!" the mother bear growls.

"My bowl is totally empty!" The father bear lets out another super-loud ROAR.

Ow, my ears!

"Who would do such a thing?" Mother Bear asks.

Father Bear looks around the house, his big dark eyes stopping on the half-open bedroom door.

"This way," he says, and he, Mother Bear, and Kid Bear all begin stomping toward us.

CRUMBS. We have to get out of here. But we're trapped. The bears didn't hurt Goldilocks in the original story, but this is *not* the original story.

Because we messed it up. As usual.

Three sets of heavy footsteps come closer. And closer. The bears are now IN the bedroom. But they don't seem to see us. Yet.

"Well, whoever was in our house is gone," Mother Bear says. She's standing right by the bed — that I'm *in*.

Please don't lift the covers. Please don't lift the covers. Please don't lift the covers.

I don't breathe. I don't move. I stay very still. I can just see out from under the edge of the blanket.

Mother Bear reaches toward the window curtains. Oh, no. Oh, no. She's going to find Goldilocks.

Mother Bear pulls the curtains back.

No one's there.

Huh?

Oh, the window is open!

Goldie must have snuck out!

She escaped!

And left us to the bears.

Gee, thanks, Goldie.

"Just wait until I catch whoever dared eat our porridge!" Father Bear hollers, his angry voice shaking the room.

Kid Bear is coming toward me. Closer. And closer. And — oh, no — lifting the covers.

AHHHHH!

I'm about to become bear breakfast. They are going to rip me to shreds and sprinkle me over their porridge like cinnamon.

I squeeze my eyes shut. I can't look.

I hear a tiny little gasp.

I open my eyes. Up close, Kid Bear is kind of cute. She looks like Berry Bear, the stuffed animal my nana gave me when I was little.

"GROOOWWWL!"

But she growls like a real bear.

Grrr! Woof! Prince barks, rushing out from underneath the biggest bed. Awww. He's trying to protect me. He does not seem to realize that even the kid bear is three times his size. She's *Jonah's* size.

"Mom! Dad!" Kid Bear yells. "There's a girl sleeping in my bed!"

That's what she said in the original story! Except this time, she's talking about *me*.

"Oh, and there's a doggie," Kid Bear adds, staring at Prince.

But Mother Bear and Father Bear are only focused on me. They come and loom over the bed. They are angry. They are growling. They are smelly. And scary.

I have to escape somehow.

Thinking fast, I throw the blanket up and over the bears, covering them so that they can't see. I jump out of bed. I grab Jonah's hand, yell, "Come on, Prince!" and run to the front door.

Prince is right behind us.

"ROAR!" Father Bear growls.

We're almost to the front door. Jonah stops to grab his skateboard, and I pull the door open and check over my shoulder to see if the bears are chasing us.

They're not.

Because the kid bear is crying. Did we scare her?

I keep running, but hear the dad bear saying, "Everything's going to be all right. Those kids can't get too far. I'll find them and teach them a lesson."

"Run!" I tell Jonah, pushing him ahead and slamming the door behind us.

We run outside. The hail has stopped. It's still cold, but at least no ice balls are bouncing off my head.

Jonah stops abruptly. I crash into him.

Ow. "Go, go, go!" I order. What's he doing?

"But look!" he says, pointing.

"At what?"

"The mailbox!"

Ohhhhhhh. The bears' mailbox is swirling with purple mist.

Which means . . . it's the portal! The mailbox is our portal home. And it's swirling! So if we jump through right now, we'll be transported back to Smithville. And the bears won't eat us.

"Let's go," Jonah says. "I don't like lessons! And I definitely don't want to learn whatever lesson the dad bear wants to teach us!"

I totally agree with him.

But . . .

I hesitate.

Jonah takes a step toward the portal.

I grab on to his arm.

"Hold up," I say. I pull him behind the mailbox to hide in case the bears come charging out of the house. Prince follows us. "Maybe we should stay. For Goldie."

"Huh? Why?" he asks. "Goldie snuck out! She's safe."

"True," I say. "But . . . *why* did she break into the bears' house in the first place? What was she looking for? Is she in trouble?"

I remember how desperate she looked. And tired. She was clearly having issues.

Did Maryrose send us here to help her?

"But the bears didn't eat her. And they're about to eat us," Jonah says. "She's fine. We're the ones in danger. Her story is done."

Is her story done?

I look at my watch. It's only 12:18 at home. That means we don't have to leave here until . . . like 4:30 tomorrow afternoon. We have plenty of time.

"Abby?" Jonah urges me. "Can we jump in the portal now?"

"I don't know," I say. I'm not sure what to do.

"But didn't Maryrose open the portal here? Doesn't she want us to come home?"

Hmm. Maybe. But it's pretty rare for Maryrose to send us home so soon in a story.

I think about the crack at the bottom of the mirror. What if that messed something up?

We both look at the mailbox. The purple mist isn't as strong as it was half a minute ago. In a few seconds, it might stop swirling altogether.

We have to decide now. Stay? Or go?

True, if we leave, we definitely won't be eaten by bears. That's a plus.

But if we leave, we also won't know what happens to Goldie. We won't be able to help her find what she was looking for.

In fairy tales, we always change the story for the better. We haven't done that yet. We haven't had a chance.

"We stay," I decide. "We find Goldie. It's the right thing to do."

I hope.

chapter six

Now You See It, Now You Don't

The good news?

The sky has cleared and gone from gray and gloomy to blue and sunny. It's less cold, and the bit of snow on the ground and trees is pretty.

Also: The bears have not followed us. At least, not yet.

The bad news? We haven't found Goldie.

But we did find her footprints in the snow. Prince sniffed them out. So we're following the footprints back up the hill.

It's so slippery. I wish I was wearing my boots. Maybe that's what Goldie was looking for. Snow boots.

"Too bad we can't sled *up* a mountain," Jonah says,

clutching his skateboard. Prince whimpers, as if in agreement.

I keep checking over my shoulder for the bears, but there's still no sign of them. Ugh. I'm worried they're going to pop out from behind a tree at any minute.

"Why were those bears even awake?" I ask. "It's winter! Shouldn't they be hibernating?"

"If they have their own food and houses, they don't need to hibernate," Jonah explains. "Bears don't hibernate in zoos."

Oh. Right.

We keep following Goldie's footsteps in the snow. And then —

"Hey, Abby," Jonah says. "The footsteps stop right by that tree."

I look at where he's pointing. He's right.

Suddenly, someone jumps out from behind the tree. Ahhh! It's one of the bears!

Oh. Phew. Never mind. It's Goldie.

"Why are you following me?" she demands, hands on hips.

"We . . ." I take a step back. "We just want to make sure you're okay."

"Really?" She narrows her eyes. I can tell she doesn't trust me. Prince barks at her, and Goldie takes a step back from him. She doesn't seem that comfortable around animals.

"Well, to be honest, we were worried something was wrong," I explain. "You were searching for something at the bears' house. Why were you there?"

"Why were *you* there?" she counters, jabbing her finger at me.

Whoa. I take a step back.

"We crashed into it by accident," Jonah answers. Which is the truth.

"Oh," she says. "Well . . ." She tosses her long hair behind her shoulder. "The bears stole a book of mine. I wanted to get it back."

"Can bears read?" Jonah asks.

Goldie stares at him. "Of course they can read. Why wouldn't they be able to read? Can you read?"

"Yes," Jonah snaps.

"Do you need help getting the book back?" I ask Goldie, trying to keep us focused.

Her eyes widen. "Uh, no."

"Goldie, if you need help, just ask," I tell her. "That's why we're here."

"Huh?" she says, looking from me to Jonah and back at me. "What do you mean?"

"I just mean that we're happy to help you," I say quickly. She doesn't need to know all about Maryrose and the magic mirror.

"What were your names again?" she asks us, still sounding suspicious.

"I'm Abby," I say. "This is Jonah, and that's Prince."

"That's right," she says. "I remember now. I'm Goldie."

She sticks out her hand and I shake it. Then she lets go.

"Maybe we should write the bears to ask for your book back," I offer. "Do you have a paper and pen?"

She stares at me for a second, then looks at the ground. "Um, no, that's okay. Maybe the bears didn't steal my book after all. I'm not sure. I have to go. Nice to meet you!" she says. "Later, gators!" Then she turns around and hurries down the hill and out of view.

Hmm.

"That was weird," Jonah says.

"Yeah," I say. "Super weird."

"If Goldie doesn't want our help," Jonah says, "should we just go home?"

"I guess so . . ."

I look down at my watch.

My wrist is empty.

Wait. Where's my watch? Wasn't I wearing my watch before? My heart races. Yeah. I was definitely wearing my watch before.

Did it fall off?

I look all around me on the ground. I don't see it.

"What's wrong?" Jonah asks.

"My watch is gone . . ." I say.

"Maybe it's buried in the snow somewhere between here and the bears' cottage."

"But how did it just fall off?" I always make sure it's on tight. I *need* that watch.

I try to think about the last time I looked at it. Was it when I was at the bears' house? Was it outside, when the mailbox-portal was swirling? I can't remember.

Did something brush against my wrist?

Hmm.

Goldie. Goldie shook my hand.

Did *Goldie* steal my watch?

Goldie said the bears stole her book. But maybe she's the one who steals things . . . ?

Argh. No wonder she made such a quick getaway and acted so sketchy!

I need my watch back. Now.

"I think Goldie stole it," I say through gritted teeth. "We have to find her."

Jonah whistles and shakes his head. "She's something, all right."

Woof! Prince agrees.

We run the way Goldie went, down the hill. My heart is beating so fast, and not just from running.

"I see her!" Jonah cries.

I look up and there she is, sprinting straight toward the metal fence we saw before, the one separating the forest from the town.

"After her!" I shout.

chapter Seven

No Dogs Allowed

Goldie leaps over the fence and runs into the town.

Jonah, Prince, and I jog up to the metal barrier. Another sign on the fence reads: PEOPLE ONLY. ROYALLY SIGNED BY THE KING OF BEBEC.

People only? That's weird. Although maybe the royal family doesn't want the bears prowling around the town. I can kind of understand that.

"What about Prince?" Jonah asks defensively. "Is he not allowed inside?"

"Maybe no one will notice him," I say, scooping up Prince and cuddling him against my chest.

"Yeah," Jonah says, offering me a boost over the fence. "Let's go get your watch back."

The town is cute and old-timey. The buildings are made of white stone, and there are shops lining the cobblestone streets. Then I see, among the crowds of people, a girl with long blond hair.

"There's Goldie!" I cry. "She just ran into that alleyway between those shops!"

Jonah puts down his skateboard and gets on. He goes zooming along the cobblestone road. Well, more like bumping along. But he's a lot faster than me, especially since I'm carrying Prince. I follow as fast as I can.

And finally, we round into the alleyway, and there she is.

Woof! Prince barks. He leaps out of my arms and runs right in front of Goldie, blocking her path.

"Hey!" she shouts. "You're not even supposed to be in the town, you gross dog! Guards, there's a gross dog here! Dog! Dog!"

"That's not a nice way to speak to Prince," Jonah counters, hopping off his skateboard. He scoops up Prince. "Besides, you're a thief! Guards, there's a thief here! Thief! Thief!"

"Shush," Goldie says, lowering her voice. "What are you talking about?" she adds, but her face is bright red.

"Did you steal my watch?" I ask her.

"No," she says, lifting her chin. But her face is still red and she won't meet my eyes.

"I think you're lying," I say.

"I . . ." She hesitates. "Fine! I did."

She admitted it! I can't believe it!

She stands there. Not moving.

Is she kidding me? "Can I have it back?"

She sighs. *"Fine!"* She reaches into her pocket and pulls out my watch. She tosses it to me. "Happy?"

Luckily, I catch it. "Um, yeah. It's MY watch!" I look at the time as I put it back on. One A.M. at home.

"Well, now you have it back," she says.

"Aren't you going to apologize?" Jonah asks.

"Why should I?" Goldie huffs.

Do we need to review the facts again? I shake my head and say, "You literally stole my watch off my wrist. And then ran away. You should apologize."

"Whatever," she huffs. "I'm sorry. But I had no choice."

"There's always a choice," I say carefully. "Do you want to tell us what's going on? Why did you steal my watch? Why were you in the bears' house? They didn't really take your book, did they?"

Her shoulders slump. "No," she says. "They didn't. It's a long story. You probably don't care."

I do my best to push away my feelings of annoyance. Why is Goldie being so difficult?

"We do care," I say. "Tell us. We want to help. For real."

Goldie takes a deep breath. "My mom died when I was little, and I live with my dad. But the king of Bebec put my dad in jail. To free him, I have to give the king a bag of gold."

"A bag of gold?" I repeat. "That's a lot of gold."

"It depends on the size of the bag," Jonah says. "Ziploc or duffel?"

"I don't know what those are," Goldie says, frowning at Jonah. "But everyone knows that a bag of gold is one hundred gold coins."

"Right . . . everyone totally knows that," Jonah says, nodding quickly.

"Why do you have to give the king any gold?" I ask. "He must be super rich. He's a king!"

"My dad worked as King Ned's assistant," Goldie explains. "And when my dad was at the palace one day, he accidentally knocked over a statue of the king. It broke into pieces. The king was mad. Really mad. He put my dad in jail and said he can only go free if he gives him a bag of gold to pay him back for the statue."

"But it was an accident," I say. "That seems kind of wrong."

"I agree," Goldie says with a tired sigh. "But that doesn't change the fact that my dad's been in jail for two weeks, and he could be there forever if I don't come up with the gold."

She looks so sad. Jonah and I exchange a glance. It's obvious that Goldie isn't lying this time.

"The king doesn't sound very nice," I say.

"Oh, he's not," Goldie says. "King Ned is awful to everyone. My dad only took the job because he had to. The king saw him in town and liked his shirt and declared him his assistant."

"Just because he liked his shirt?" I ask.

Goldie nods. "It was a really cool shirt. It had blue and green stripes and polka dots . . ." She shakes her head. "Beside the point. My dad didn't want the job. All the king's assistants end up in jail. But *no one* refuses the king. My dad used to be a carpenter."

"Is there a queen?" I ask. "Is she as bad as the king is?"

Goldie shrugs. "She's pretty quiet. She wasn't always a royal. When the king gives his speeches from the grand palace tower, she just stands beside him and listens like everyone else. Sometimes I think she forgets she's the queen."

"So she can't help us," I say.

"No," Goldie says, and covers her face with her hands. "What am I going to do? I'm running out of food, and options. I know stealing is wrong. I never want to hurt anyone. But I'm only taking stuff to sell for food and save up the coins for my dad. And I've mostly been stealing from the animals. That's allowed in Bebec."

"Seriously?" Jonah asks.

Goldie nods. "The law in the kingdom is that you can't steal from people. But you can steal from the animals. King Ned doesn't care about the animals at all."

"The forest isn't part of Bebec?" I ask.

"Oh, it is," Goldie responds. "Bebec is divided into three sections. The forest, where the animals live. The town, where the people live. And the palace, where the royal family and their servants live."

She turns and points to the huge gray castle in the distance.

"Do all the animals live in houses?" Jonah asks.

Goldie laughs. "Don't be silly. Just the bears. And the foxes."

"What about dogs?" I ask, looking at Prince.

"Now you're really being ridiculous," she says. "Ha! We don't even have dogs in Bebec! They all moved to the neighboring kingdom, Montario."

Prince looks offended.

"Anyway, I hadn't been to the Bear family house before," Goldie goes on. "I slid a note under their door this morning saying that a local store had honey. That way, I knew they'd leave. But still I found nothing!"

Jonah's eyes widen. "You faked a honey sale to get them out of the house?"

She shrugs. "I was desperate."

"Did you steal anything from them?" I ask.

"No," she says. "I didn't have a chance."

That's good at least.

"I'm sorry for everything you've been through," I say. Poor Goldie. Now that she's opened up to us a little, I'm starting to like her more. And it's awful that she's cold and hungry, and desperate to get her dad out of jail.

She kicks at the cobblestone in the alleyway. "You said you'd help me if I needed it. And I do need help. So are you going to help me or not?"

"I . . ." I look at Jonah.

He wrinkles his nose.

"You're not going to help me? Fine!" Goldie snaps. "Then don't waste my time!" She turns and marches off, her curly hair bouncing. Prince barks after her.

"Why don't you want to help her?" I whisper to Jonah.

He twists his lip. "How do we know we can trust her? She stole your watch!"

True. "But she stole it to sell it for gold," I point out. "To get her dad out of jail."

Jonah shrugs. "Maybe. Or maybe she's lying again."

Usually Jonah's the one who trusts people and I'm the one who needs convincing. "I don't get the feeling she's lying this time. Why would she make up a story like that?"

"Uh, to get gold?"

"But if her dad *is* in jail, we should help get him out." I think about Maryrose, trapped in our mirror. How would she feel if we didn't help someone who was trapped?

"I guess," Jonah says. "Although we could get stuck in this story forever."

"We've never gotten stuck anywhere forever before," I say. "Although the mirror has never been broken before."

"It isn't broken," Jonah says. "It's just . . . cracked."

Suuuuuure.

"How do we help, anyway?" Jonah asks. "Are we going to help her steal gold?"

"No," I say. "Of course not. But help her find gold, maybe. Are you okay with that?"

Jonah thinks for a minute, then nods.

"Okay," I say. "Let's catch up to her again before we lose her for good."

With Prince tucked in Jonah's arms, we hurry through the crowded streets until we spot Goldie walking along a row of shops. She's staring into a grocery store window with longing.

"Goldie!" I call.

She looks over and frowns. "You two again? If you're not going to help, just go."

"We *are* going to help," I tell her. "Promise."

Goldie eyes us up and down. She seems to be thinking things over.

"I guess it can't hurt," she finally says. "It's not like you can make things any worse."

Thanks for the vote of support. "Why don't we go sit down somewhere to brainstorm ideas?" I suggest.

Goldie yawns. "Good idea. Should we go to your house?"

Jonah and I exchange a glance. "Um . . . why don't we go to yours?" I ask.

"Because you think I'm going to steal from you?" she asks huffily.

"No," I say. "Maybe. But that's not why. We just, um, live very far away. Can we go to your house?"

"Fine," she says a little grumpily. "Come on."

chapter eight

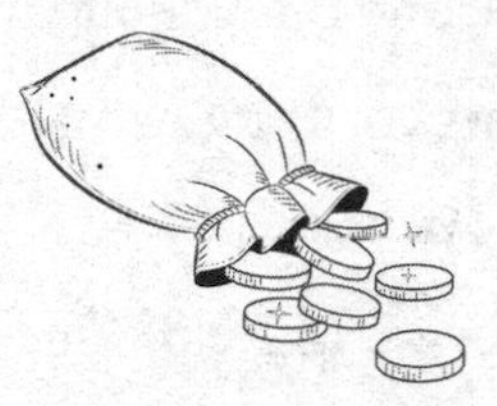

Two In One

We follow Goldie down a bunch of cobblestone streets and alleyways until we reach a stone cottage with a round orange door. There's peeling paint on the windowsills and the mat is all scuffed, but something about the house seems friendly. There's a small backyard with trees and a shed.

Goldie lets us inside the cottage. It's tiny but clean. The living room has a lumpy tan sofa with flat brown pillows. The rug looks worn. There are no decorations at all.

"I sold everything I could," Goldie explains. "But what little money I got for our stuff, I had to use for food."

I swallow hard. Now I'm definitely glad we decided to help Goldie.

Jonah sets Prince and his skateboard down on the floor. Prince curls up on the worn rug, while Jonah and I sit beside Goldie on the lumpy couch.

"Thanks for offering to help," she says. "I'm sorry if I was rude. I'm just . . . stressed."

"We completely understand," I say. "And we're for sure going to help. You need a bag of gold. So let's find gold."

"But where?" she asks. "No one has much money in Bebec. I can't borrow it, and no one will hire me for a job. I've asked in every shop and restaurant!"

Hmm. We've had to earn money in fairy tales before. When we fell into the story of *Cinderella*, we baked and sold brownies in town. But since no one in that kingdom had ever heard of brownies, we called them crownies. And Cinderella made a lot of money selling them and even opened her own bakery, called Cinderella's Crownies.

I am a big fan of alliteration.

I feel a spark of excitement. Maybe they don't have brownies in Bebec, either! We could do that again! We could even change the name to something with a G. Grownies! Goldie's Grownies! Hmm. That sounds kind of gross, actually. Kind of like you're eating the ground. Or worms.

Goldie's . . . Gummies? Glownies? I'll have to keep thinking.

"Listen up," I announce, rubbing my hands together. "I don't have the name down just yet, but I think we should bake delicious chocolate fudgy cakes. Where we come from they're called brownies and people love them!"

Goldie rolls her eyes. "Yeah. People love them here, too. Everyone makes brownies."

Oh.

Okay, forget brownies. Though of course now I wish I had one.

"What about cupcakes?" Jonah asks.

"I don't want to talk about cupcakes," I say, grimacing. I'm still upset about my baking disaster.

"We have cupcakes in Bebec, too," Goldie says.

"Cookies?" I suggest.

"Yep."

Hmmm.

"I could really use something sweet right now," Jonah says. "Since *someone* never gave me a cupcake back home. I'm hungry."

"I don't have anything sweet," Goldie says. "Sorry."

"Oh!" Jonah says. "I know. Cake pops! I bet Bebec doesn't have those! Those are newish."

"We have cake pops," Goldie says with a sigh. "We've had them forever."

"Maybe we should move on from baked goods," I say. "Would you start a band?" I suggest.

"And put on concerts!" Jonah adds. "Like in *Rapunzel*!"

"Exactly," I say.

"What's Rapunzel?" Goldie asks.

"Nothing," Jonah and I say.

"Are you a good singer?" Jonah asks, changing the subject.

"Yeah! At least that's what my dad always tells me," Goldie says. "I'll sing the Bebec national anthem for you."

We wait as she stands and clears her throat. I'm already thinking of printing concert T-shirts to sell and —

She starts to sing. "Oh, Bebec! A pl*ace* most bea*utiful* —" Her voice cracks on the *ace*. And then again on the *utiful*.

Do you know what's not beautiful? Her voice.

She stops. "What? You don't like that song? It's a classic."

Jonah coughs. "It's not the song that's the problem."

"Really?" she asks, surprised. "Is my dad just being nice?"

"Yes," Jonah says, wincing. "You do not have a good voice. Sorry! We don't, either!"

"Speak for yourself," I say, and Jonah snorts.

"Okay, I don't have a good voice, either," I admit.

"So none of us are getting rich off singing professionally," Goldie says.

"Nope," I agree. "Can you sew?"

"No," she says.

"Draw?"

"Barely," she says.

"Do magic tricks?" Jonah asks.

I laugh. "Really?"

"Why not?" he asks. "I'd pay to see magic tricks."

"I cannot do magic tricks," Goldie says.

"The only magician I'd pay to see right now is one who could turn stuff into gold," I say. "Like Rumpelstiltskin."

Goldie sighs. "Rumpelstiltskin would never help," she says. "Everyone says he's a jerk."

"Yeah," I say. "I've heard that, too. Anyway, we need to keep brainstorming. Goldie, what do you want to do when you grow up?"

"Why?"

"Maybe it will inspire us. For instance, I want to be a judge."

"Oh. Well, I've always thought it would be fun to run my own business."

Wait a sec.

Wait. A. Sec.

"Goldie!" I cry. "What did you just say?"

"That I want to run my own business." Her cheeks flush. "What, you don't think I can do it?"

"Not that!" I jump off the couch. "Before! You said Rumpelstiltskin would never help! You said he was a jerk! You've heard of Rumpelstiltskin?"

"Of course. He lives in the forest somewhere. Do you know him?"

"He's *here*?" I ask. "In Bebec?"

"Yes," she responds.

I look at Jonah. Jonah looks at me. It must be a different Rumpelstiltskin. Right?

But how many Rumpelstiltskins can there be? It's not exactly a common name. It's not like my class has two Rumpelstiltskins, Rumpelstiltskin S. and Rumpelstiltskin D. Although if my name was Rumpelstiltskin, I would probably insist on a nickname like Rumpy or Skins. Maybe Stilts.

Stiltsy is kind of cute.

"Do you think it's the same one?" Jonah asks me.

"Is that possible? Could there be more than one?" I answer.

No. We're in the story of *Goldilocks and the Three Bears*. Not the story of *Rumpelstiltskin*. Would he really be in this story? That is so . . . messy! Each story is distinct! Each story stays in its own lane. Each story is *just right* the way it is. There's no two-in-one.

Is there?

"I don't remember the *Rumpelstiltskin* story at all," Jonah says.

"You never remember the stories," I say. Our nana used to read them all to us. Jonah did not always pay attention. Since we found our magic mirror in our basement, I've been reading the fairy tales on my own to make sure I know as much as possible about any story I could potentially fall into.

"What are you two even talking about?" Goldie finally calls out, throwing up her hands.

"Just, um, what I know about Rumpelstiltskin's background," I say quickly. "Tell me if this sounds like the guy who lives here?"

She leans forward. "Okay. Go for it."

"There's this miller —"

"A what?" Jonah asks.

"A miller is someone who operates a mill — grinds wheat or corn into flour."

"Got it," he says, and gives me a thumbs-up.

"This miller was hanging around a king one day, and he was kind of bragging. And he told the king his daughter could turn straw into gold."

"Could she?" Goldie asks. "That would be useful."

"No," I say. "She couldn't."

"Why would her father say that, then?" Jonah asks. "Seems risky."

"Unclear," I say. "Anyway! The king said, 'Great, if she can do that, I want her working for me.' Then the king locked her in a room with straw, and said if she couldn't spin the straw into gold by morning she would have to die."

"Oh, snap," Goldie says, eyes wide. "That's harsh."

"It totally is," Jonah says.

"Right? The miller's daughter cried and cried, and then as she was crying, a little man named Rumpelstiltskin snuck inside. The miller's daughter didn't know his name, though. That's important. Rumpelstiltskin offered to turn the straw into gold if she gave him something. She offered him her necklace. He accepted and did it."

"He did?" Goldie squeals. "Cool!"

"Yup. Except, then the king came into the room and was thrilled. But he was also greedy. So he brought the miller's daughter to another room with even more straw in it and told her to do it again."

"Ugh," Jonah says.

"Right. So the whole thing happened again, and this time the miller's daughter offered Rumpelstiltskin her ring. And he spun all the straw into gold again."

"Hurrah!" Jonah says.

Goldie narrows her eyes. "I'm not cheering just yet. I bet something bad happens. King Ned is one greedy guy."

King Ned? Could it be? Rumpelstiltskin's king is the same as Goldilocks's king? Whoa.

"Anyway," I go on, "the king was so impressed with all his gold that he put the miller's daughter in *another* room of straw and he said if she did it again, he would marry her and make her the queen. But when Rumpelstiltskin came back and offered to help her again, she had nothing left to give him."

"So what happened?" Jonah asked.

"Rumpelstiltskin said that if she did marry the king, and if she had a baby, she had to give the baby to him."

"Yikes," Goldie says. "What did he want with a baby?"

"Maybe he wanted to eat it," Jonah says.

"Why would someone want to eat a baby?" I ask, shaking my head.

"Why did Snow White's stepmom want to eat her heart?" Jonah retorts. "Or why did Cinderella's stepsisters cut off parts of their feet? People in fairy tales do disgusting things."

"True," I say. "But maybe he just wanted a baby. Like to have. Maybe he was lonely."

"So what happened?" Goldie asks. "She didn't agree, did she?"

"What choice did she have?" I ask. "She didn't want the king to kill her. She agreed to the terms. She probably thought she could get out of it later."

"Did she?" Goldie asks.

"No. So the miller's daughter ended up marrying the king because he loved having a queen who could make gold. He had no idea it was really Rumpelstiltskin who did that. And then a year later she got pregnant. And then after the king and queen had a baby, Rumpelstiltskin appeared and told the queen to hand over the child as agreed."

Goldie whistles. "Oh, no."

I nod. "The queen was upset. Obviously. She begged Rumpelstiltskin to reconsider. She offered him anything instead. But he wanted nothing else from her."

"Because he was hungry! He wanted a baby sandwich," Jonah says.

"Jonah! No. Probably not. Anyway, Rumpelstiltskin felt bad for her and told her that if she could guess his name, she could keep her baby. No one in the entire kingdom knew what his name was."

"It's not a very common name," Jonah says. "How would she ever guess it?"

"That's what Rumpelstiltskin was counting on," I say. "But one day, someone overheard him singing a song with his name in it and told the queen what his name was. Rumpelstiltskin was mad! Since he lost the baby —"

"Baby sandwich," Jonah laughs.

"Gross," I say, but Goldie giggles and then I laugh, too.

"Rumpelstiltskin stormed off. And that's the end of the sandwich," I say. "I mean story!"

Now all three of us are laughing.

I turn to Goldie. "Can you tell us what you know about Rumpelstiltskin? Does that story match up with what you've heard? Is it the same guy?"

Goldie nods. "I've heard about an elf named Rumpelstiltskin who got into a fight with the king and queen about something involving straw. He's been hiding from them in the forest ever since."

"That matches up," I say. "I guess he's an elf."

"Wow," Jonah says to me. "That means we're really in two fairy tales — in one!"

"What's a fairy tale?" Goldie asks.

"It's a long story," Jonah says.

"A fairy tale is a long story?" Goldie asks, confused.

"No, a fairy tale is a short story," Jonah says. "Or sometimes a long story. It's a story."

"With fairies?" Goldie asks, looking back and forth between us.

"Sometimes," Jonah says.

"We've never been in two before," I say. "How could that have happened?"

Wait. A. Minute.

The mirror! "The crack," I say.

Jonah cringes. "Oops."

"No kidding," I sigh.

He leans forward. "Or maybe yay. If it helps us."

I nod. Hmm. "It could be good."

"What could be good?" Goldie asks. "What are you two *talking* about?"

I turn to her and smile. "We know how to get you the gold."

chapter nine

Finding Rumpy

"You're saying we just have to find Rumpelstiltskin," Goldie says after I explain my plan.

"Exactly," I say.

"But nobody knows where he lives," she says.

"That will definitely make it harder," Jonah says.

"The animals might know," Goldie says, considering. "But they won't tell us. They don't like that the human residents are treated better by the king. They're not even truly considered part of Bebec. That's why they live in the forest and we live in the town."

This king really is the worst.

"Do all the animals talk?" Jonah asks.

"Of course," she says.

Prince barks.

Not all.

"Maybe if we ask the animals nicely they'll help us," I suggest. "If they dislike the king, too, maybe they'll be on our side. Isn't the enemy of our enemy our friend?" I think I heard that expression once.

Goldie shrugs. "We can try. But don't count on it."

Prince walks over to Goldie and sits by her foot. He stares up at her. I think he's waiting for her to pet him.

Goldie sort of scowls at him.

Hmm. She's not really an animal person.

"You can pet him if you want," I say. "He loves scratches behind the ears and belly rubs."

She scrunches up her face. "Uh, no, thanks."

Poor Prince.

"You don't like dogs?" Jonah asks, bending down to scratch Prince behind his ears.

"I'm a people person," she says.

Is she? She doesn't seem that great with people, either.

Jonah's stomach growls, and mine does, too. And so does Goldie's.

"Any chance you have anything to eat for lunch?" Jonah asks.

"No," Goldie says. "And unlike you two, I didn't even get breakfast. But if we're going to find the animals, we need to go back into the forest, and there are some apple trees there. Do you like apples?"

"Everyone likes apples," I say.

"Except Snow White," Jonah says.

Ha.

Jonah scoops up his skateboard and Prince, and we all leave Goldie's cottage. We walk through the town back to the fence, and cross over into the forest.

"Animals!" Jonah hollers. "Hello! Any animals there? We could use your help!"

Silence.

"Were you really expecting that to work?" Goldie asks.

"Kind of," he says.

Prince barks twice and then runs toward a tree. He barks at the tree twice more, looking up.

"What do you see there?" I ask Prince. "An animal? Or an apple?"

"I'll take an apple," Goldie says.

"Ow!" Jonah says, rubbing his head.

"What happened?" I ask, turning toward him.

"Something bonked me on the head!" Jonah says.

"Was it an apple?" I ask.

Jonah feels around his mop of brown curly hair. He pulls out an acorn. "Nope. We can't eat acorns, can we?" he asks.

We all look up at the tree Prince is barking at. There's a furry gray squirrel with amber-colored eyes sitting on a branch. She's wearing a tiny green dress.

"Sorry. I dropped my acorn by accident," the squirrel says. It's a little weird to see a squirrel talk, but no weirder than talking bears. "All that barking startled me."

Good job, Prince! He might not be able to talk, but he can certainly help.

Hmm. I wonder if Prince feels weird that he is the only animal in the story not talking and not wearing clothes. Do I need to find him a doggie sweatsuit or something?

Jonah holds the acorn up to the squirrel. "Here you go."

"Thanks!" the squirrel says.

"Excuse me, Squirrel?" I ask. "Would you help us with something?"

"That's *Ms.* Squirrel to you."

"Sorry. Ms. Squirrel? Would you help us with something?"

She frowns. "Well, you did retrieve my acorn for me. What do you need?"

"Do you know where Rumpelstiltskin's house is?" I ask.

The end of the squirrel's tail twitches from under her dress. "I'm not entirely sure where he lives. But apparently he's very peculiar."

"Yes," I say. "We've heard that, too."

"Are you sure you want to talk to him?"

I nod. "Yes, please."

"I've heard it's up the mountain and near some water," she says.

I look up the mountain, the same one Jonah and I slid down on his skateboard.

"Well, that's more information than we had before," I say.

"Good luck," Ms. Squirrel says, and jumps to another branch.

I glance at Jonah and Goldie. "I guess we go back up the mountain." I take a deep breath.

"Onward and upward," Jonah says, and we head off.

We hike up the mountain. We pass by trees. And more trees.

"This looks familiar," Jonah says.

"Because we're standing exactly where we were when we first went through the mirror and landed in Goldie's story," I say.

"Oh!" Jonah exclaims, looking around. "Right!"

"But where is Rumpelstiltskin?" Goldie asks. By now she's stopped asking us what we mean when we talk about landing in stories. I think she thinks we're just weird.

"Hello?" I call out. "Rumpelstiltskin? Are you there? Do you hear us? We'd love to talk to you!"

There's silence. And then —

"ROAR!"

We all freeze. Prince flattens his ears. Uh-oh. I know that roar.

"Abby!" Jonah whisper-yells. "That sounded like a bear roar!"

I nod. Unfortunately, it did. The dad bear said he would come after us, and he did!

I try to remember what I learned at camp about meeting a bear in the woods. Do you run or play dead?

"ROAR!" we hear again.

And then I see the bear burst through the trees.

AHHHH! I cover my eyes with my hands and peek through my splayed fingers.

But it's not Father Bear who jumps out of the trees.

Or Mother Bear.

It's Kid Bear. She's still in her orange jumpsuit and pink tutu.

I brace myself for impact. She might be a cub, but her teeth and nails are still razor sharp.

"Hi!" Kid Bear says.

"Um, hi?" I say back. She does not seem to be interested in attacking us.

"You're the girl who was sleeping in my bed," she adds, her big brown eyes on me.

I swallow.

"Sorry about that," I say. "Your bed looked so comfortable."

"It really is," the baby bear says. "It's just right!"

I laugh. I can't help it.

I look at Kid Bear. I tilt my head. She tilts hers. She doesn't seem angry at all. She seems kind of . . . happy and friendly.

"And you're the boy with the skateboard," the bear says to Jonah. "And the dog."

"Um . . . yeah?" Jonah says, holding his skateboard and Prince protectively.

Goldie takes a tentative step toward Kid Bear. "Have you been following us?" she asks.

Kid Bear nods. "I wanted to meet the boy and girl who came over. We've never had people in our house before."

"You've never had anyone in your house before?" Jonah asks.

"No, we've never had *people*. Or dogs. My parents say people are mean. But you didn't seem that mean. You seemed kind of scared."

"We were scared," I say.

"I wasn't scared, I just had things to do," Goldie says. "And I still have things to do. So if you're not going to eat us, can we move this along?"

"Do you happen to know where Rumpelstiltskin's house is?" I ask Kid Bear.

"I do," she says. "I followed him once. I follow people a lot. And elves. Just for fun. I can show you where. He lives behind a waterfall. That one." She turns and points to the frozen waterfall that I saw when we first landed in the story. Wow!

Goldie rolls her eyes. "Sure. Because that's where people live. Behind waterfalls. Frozen waterfalls, at that. Please."

"Rumpelstiltskin has magic powers," Jonah reminds Goldie. "Also, he's an elf."

"It's true," I say. "He could live behind a waterfall."

"He really does!" Kid Bear says earnestly. "I'll lead you over to it."

"How do we know we can trust you?" Goldie asks her. "What if you just want us to follow you and then you're going to eat us?"

"No offense," Kid Bear says, "but if I wanted to eat you, I would have done it already. Besides, my family and I don't eat people. We eat porridge, honey, mac and cheese, and vanilla cupcakes."

Cupcakes. Obviously.

"How do we know you're not just trying to get us into one place and then trap us?" Goldie demands.

"Will you excuse us for a moment, Kid Bear?" I ask.

"Sure," she says, sitting down crisscross applesauce on the ground.

"Goldie," I whisper. "Can Jonah and I talk to you?"

"Fine," Goldie says.

We all go behind a huge tree trunk.

"Let's run," Goldie says.

"Wait, why don't you believe Kid Bear?" I ask.

"Because she's a *bear*!" Goldie says, exasperated. "Animals are not to be believed." Prince lets out a huffy bark. "Everyone knows that. Especially the bears and foxes who live in houses in Bebec Forest. They're extra mad that they can't go into the town."

"Well, they should be extra mad," Jonah points out.

"No," Goldie says. "They don't deserve it. Anyway, I don't trust her. She might be pretending to be nice."

I raise an eyebrow. "Like you were?"

"Yes. Exactly. Maybe all the animals are working together to set us up!"

"Sounds like you don't trust them because they're animals and not people," Jonah says.

"So?" Goldie counters.

"So," Jonah says, "you should decide who to trust based on what you *know*, not what you *think* you know."

She rolls her eyes again. "You guys are annoying. I've said what I had to say."

"Let's take a vote," Jonah says. "All in favor of following the bear to Rumpelstiltskin's?"

He and I raise our hands. Prince wags his tail.

"Whatever," Goldie says. "Don't blame me if we get eaten."

"We won't!" Jonah says cheerfully.

We return to Kid Bear, who's still sitting patiently on the ground.

"Okay, we're ready. Lead us to Rumpelstiltskin's house," I say.

"Yay!" she says, bouncing up. "I get to help. Come on!" And she goes running on all fours through the big stand of evergreens.

We all follow her along a path through the trees. As we come around a bend, we stop — and we all gasp.

The waterfall is incredible. A huge swath of water is

completely frozen over the edge of the cliff, ending in a frozen lake below. It looks even cooler up close than it did from far away.

"Maybe the bears will freeze us and save us as a summer snack," Goldie whispers. "Kid sandwich."

Jonah laughs. I decide to ignore her. "How do we get to the house?" I ask. "Does anyone see a house?"

"It's *behind* the waterfall," Kid Bear says. "That's why you don't see it."

"Do we have to ice-skate to the door?" I ask.

"No, we have to climb the rocks on the side and then take the stone ledge behind the waterfall to find the door." She starts climbing. "Come on!"

"Um, Kid Bear? We don't have sharp claws to climb rocks," I say. "Since we're people."

"How cool would that be, though?" Jonah sighs. "I wish Mom didn't make me cut my toenails."

"That is disgusting," Goldie says.

"Yeah, Jonah," I say, with a laugh.

"Just grab on to the grooves in the rock with your hands," Kid Bear says.

Jonah nods. He's actually a great rock climber. He tucks

his skateboard and Prince under his arm and starts climbing. He's halfway up the rocks by the time I find my first groove. I grab on.

"Be careful," I call up to him.

"I am!"

Woof! Prince barks.

"You too, Goldie," I add, glancing over my shoulder. "You're coming, right?"

"Um . . ." She looks up. "Maybe?"

"You can do it!" I tell her.

"I know I can," she says. "I just don't know if I want to."

"Come on, Goldie," I say, my patience waning. I try not to twist to look down at her so I don't slip. "We're doing this for you, you know."

She sighs again. "You're right. I'm sorry. I'm coming."

I give her a quick thumbs-up and keep going. I'm not a big fan of heights, but this isn't too bad. I grab on to openings in the rock and hoist myself up, finally making it onto the ledge, with Goldie right behind me. Jonah, Prince, and Kid Bear are waiting for us.

"What took ya so long?" Kid Bear asks.

Jonah laughs.

The frozen waterfall is even more beautiful on this side. It's like looking at a stained-glass wall, but one made of sparkling diamonds.

"There it is," Jonah says. "The door!"

I turn around very carefully. Jonah is right. There is a door built right into the stone. It's barely noticeable. There's no handle.

I'm not a million percent sure, but . . .

I think we found Rumpelstiltskin's house!

chapter ten

The House

"You were right!" I say to Kid Bear.

Her furry brown chest puffs up with pride, and she does a shimmy. "Told you," she says.

"We don't know that yet," Goldie points out. "Someone should knock and see if Rumpelstiltskin answers."

Tough customer.

"I wish I lived behind a waterfall," Jonah says. "So awesome."

It *is* very cool. No wonder no one knows exactly where he lives. Who would ever think to look behind a waterfall?

I'm about to knock on the door when something occurs to me.

"Wait. If Rumpelstiltskin can make gold, why wouldn't he live in a huge, fancy house?"

"A huge fancy house made of gold," Goldie says.

"I'd rather live in this small house behind the waterfall," Jonah says.

"Rumpelstiltskin is pretty little," Kid Bear says. "He definitely doesn't need a big house."

"Let's knock!" Jonah says. "I want to meet him."

I'm suddenly worried. Rumpelstiltskin wasn't the nicest in his story. He tried to swindle the queen out of her baby! But what choice do we have?

I take a deep breath and then knock on the front door.

"Who is it?" a high-pitched voice calls from inside.

"Abby!" I call.

"And Jonah," Jonah adds.

"And Goldie," Goldie says.

"And Kid Bear!" I add. That's probably not her actual name, but there's no time to ask her now.

Prince barks.

A tiny square window on the door slides open. I see two brown-orange eyes staring at us. Then the window closes. And the door opens.

Rumpelstiltskin stands in the doorway. He's about Jonah's height, with pale green skin. His brown eyes have a strange orange glow, and his hair is short and bright white. He's wearing a dark blue velvet suit and a tall, dark blue velvet hat sits on his head. With his bright white beard, he looks a little like a garden gnome.

He also looks very surprised to see us. "Why are you here?" he asks.

"We have a favor to ask you," I say.

"Do you know who I am?" he asks.

"Yes," I answer.

"So what's my name, then?" he demands, hands on hips. "I bet you can't guess. I'll give you three guesses before I slam the door on you."

"Is it . . . Jeff?" Jonah asks, a gleam in his eye.

"No!" Rumpelstiltskin calls out. "It is not! Two more guesses!"

Jonah grins. "Cody?"

Where is he coming up with these names?

"No!" Rumpelstiltskin yells.

"Jonah, come on!" I turn to Rumpelstiltskin. "We know your name. It's Rumpelstiltskin," I say.

He narrows his orange-brown eyes at me. "Well, obviously, *she* told you," Rumpelstiltskin says, now glaring at Kid Bear.

"I didn't tell them," Kid Bear insists. "They knew who you were already."

"Really?" he asks, looking from me to Jonah to Goldie and back to me.

I nod. "You're pretty famous outside of Bebec," I tell him.

"I am?" He lifts his chin and looks a lot happier. "That's nice to hear. No one ever stops by."

"Same at our house," Kid Bear says sadly. "I don't have any friends."

"Me either," Goldie says. "Now that my dad's gone, I'm all alone."

"Can we get back to your name?" Jonah asks. "Do you have a nickname? Or do you actually want to be called Rumpelstiltskin?"

"What would I use for a nickname?" he asks.

"Rumpy? Skins?" Jonah asks.

"Stiltsy?" I say.

"Hard pass," Rumpelstiltskin says. "Do you have a nickname?" he asks my brother.

Jonah shakes his head. "But you can call me Jo!"

"Does anyone ever call you that?" I ask my brother.

"Nope," he says. "But I could start using it!"

"How about a different nickname? Like . . . Nah?" I suggest.

"No," Jonah says firmly.

"Sweetie?"

"No, thank you!"

"I wish someone would call me Sweetie," Rumpelstiltskin says sadly. He shakes his head. "Would you all like to come in?"

Oh!

Jonah claps. "Yes! Cool! I'm going into Rumpelstiltskin's house!"

"Woot woot!" says Kid Bear.

Rumpelstiltskin stares at Kid Bear with surprise. "Woot woot?"

"Woot woot!" she replies.

"We'd love to come in," I say.

Rumpelstiltskin opens the door wide and we walk into a very fancy, huge house. Wow! The floors are made of shiny blue marble and there's a leather armchair, fluffy shag rugs, and a blue velvet sofa that matches his suit. From the outside, you'd never know the inside was so big and luxurious.

Our host gestures at the blue sofa, and Goldie, Jonah, Kid Bear, and I all sit down, with Prince in my lap. Rumpelstiltskin sits on the huge leather armchair across from us.

He crosses his tiny legs. "What do you want?" he asks, cutting right to the chase.

"Do you have any cookies?" Jonah asks. "I've been really in the mood for something sweet."

"I do, actually," Rumpelstiltskin says. "One minute."

He dashes off and returns a moment later holding a tray with four cups of milk, a loaf of banana bread sliced into pieces, and some cookies. Yum! Rumpelstiltskin is clearly a good baker. Too bad I didn't meet him *before* I made my ruined cupcakes.

"There are chocolate chip and oatmeal raisin cookies," Rumpelstiltskin says, holding the tray out to us.

"Hurrah!" Jonah cheers. "No thank you on the raisin,

though. Blargh. Nothing worse than biting into what you think is chocolate chip and getting raisin."

"I hate when that happens," I sigh.

"Me too," Goldie says, laughing. "But for me it's the reverse. It's oatmeal raisin that's my favorite kind of cookie."

I don't even know what to say to that.

"I like every kind of cookie," Rumpelstiltskin says.

Goldie carefully selects an oatmeal raisin cookie and a piece of banana bread. Kid Bear takes one of each cookie, and Jonah and I take one chocolate chip cookie apiece. Then Goldie takes some more banana bread, and we all help ourselves to the glasses of milk. We thank him, and Rumpelstiltskin looks pleased as he settles back into his armchair.

"So," I say to Rumpelstiltskin, biting into my cookie. "We need your help. Goldie's dad used to work in the palace as King Ned's assistant, but he broke a statue of the king by accident," I explain. "The king threw him in jail because he can't pay for it."

"What a meanie!" Kid Bear says.

Goldie nods. "He really is."

"And the only way that Goldie can free her dad is by giving the king a bag of gold," Jonah adds.

"Can you help, Rumpelstiltskin?" Goldie asks. "Please?"

He nods right away. "Of course I can help."

"Yay!" I cry. "You're the best! I knew you would. I knew it! See, Goldie?"

Rumpelstiltskin taps his fingertips together. "I said I *can*. Whether or not I *will* is the question."

I deflate like a leaking balloon.

"But you can turn things into gold," Jonah says. "It's easy for you."

Rumpelstiltskin shrugs. "So?"

"My father is in jail for an accident," Goldie says. "The king has no mercy!"

"That's true," Rumpelstiltskin agrees. "I'm magical and even I avoid his royal cruelness."

"So are you going to help or not?" Goldie asks.

"Please?" I say. He has to!

"Double please with rainbow sprinkles on top?" Jonah adds.

"I love rainbow sprinkles," Kid Bear says, licking her lips.

Rumpelstiltskin looks at us all one by one. Then he taps his chin. "All right," he says. "I'll help."

Hurrah!

"Here's what you have to do," he goes on. "Bring me straw. And lots of it."

The straw part makes sense. That's what he turned to gold in his story.

"Can't you turn anything into gold?" Jonah asks.

Rumpelstiltskin shakes his head and his hat goes flying off. He grumbles and hops down off the big chair, puts the hat on, then hops back up. "No," he says. "Just straw."

"Okay, so we have to find straw —" I start.

"And of course," Rumpelstiltskin adds, "you'll have to pay me."

Goldie frowns. I swallow. Jonah bites his lip. Even Kid Bear looks worried.

"We don't have any money," I say. "That's why we need you to turn straw into gold!"

"Did I ask for money?" Rumpelstiltskin bellows. "No, I did not."

I stare at him. "Then what do you want in exchange? We have a skateboard. Want that?"

"No!" Jonah yells.

"Jonah!" I say. "It's all we have!"

"We have your watch!"

"We need my watch!"

"Well, I need my skateboard!"

"I don't want a skateboard *or* a watch," Rumpelstiltskin says.

"What do you want?" I ask.

"Your firstborn child!" he declares.

"Um, no," I say. "First of all, I'm way too young to have kids. And second of all, I'm not auctioning off any future kids that I might have."

Rumpelstiltskin frowns. He looks at Jonah. "Then *his* firstborn child!" he declares.

"Also no," Jonah says, and then mutters, "Baby sandwich" under his breath.

"You can't have any of our firstborn children," I say. "Not mine, not Jonah's, not Goldie's, not Kid Bear's."

He squishes his face up. "What about your second-born children?" he asks.

"No," I say.

"Last-born?"

"Still no," I say. "No kids of any kind."

"Can I have your dog?" he asks.

"No dog, either," I say, pulling Prince closer to me. "Or my dog's puppies. Just to make it clear — no living being."

Rumpelstiltskin sighs. "It would be so nice to have a friend."

"A friend sandwich," Jonah mutters.

"Jonah, stop," I say. "He doesn't want a person sandwich. He wants a companion. He's lonely. Aren't you?"

Rumpelstiltskin's orange-brown eyes fill with tears. "I am. I just want companionship. I don't understand why no one wants to hang out with me!"

"Maybe it's because you try to steal people's babies?" Jonah asks.

He scowls. "I never stole anything. I made deals. And anyway, that's only when I'm desperate. And the thing is, I'm not very happy. The only time anyone talks to me is when they want my help." He sighs again, his eyes filling with more tears.

Awww. Poor Rumpy.

"Rumpelstiltskin?" I say. "Will you excuse us for a moment?"

"Fine," he says, sniffling and wiping his eyes.

He hops off the chair and goes into another room.

"Goldie and Kid Bear," I whisper. "I have an idea. *You* both want friends, right?" They nod. "And Rumpelstiltskin needs a friend. Maybe the three of you can be friends?"

Goldie and Kid Bear look at each other.

"It's like *Goldie and Bear*!" Jonah exclaims. "That cartoon. Except in this case, it's Goldie and Bear and Rumpelstiltskin." He pauses. "That doesn't have quite the same ring."

"I don't know," Goldie says, studying Kid Bear. "You're an animal, so I shouldn't be nice to you, but you *did* help us find Rumpelstiltskin. And your tutu is kind of cool."

"Thanks," Kid Bear says. "You're hanging out with the people who broke into my house, but you seem pretty cool, too."

"Oh," Goldie says. "About that . . . I broke into your house, too. I'm really sorry. I was looking for ways to help my dad. I know it was wrong." She lowers her head. "Can you forgive me?"

Kid Bear nods. "I can. I've always wanted to be friends with a person." She pauses and smiles at Goldie. "I'll be your friend."

Yay!

"But what about Rumpelstiltskin?" I ask.

"I guess it'd be fun to have a magical elf friend," Goldie responds. "Plus, I do need his help."

Jonah leans close. "Goldie, if you want to be his friend," he says, "it can't be because you need his help. Friends are friends because they like each other."

"I can't say I *like* him yet," Goldie says. "I barely know him. But I am willing to hang out with him."

"I want to be friends with everyone!" Kid Bear exclaims.

I can't help but smile. Kid Bear is kind of the best.

"Can I come back now?" Rumpelstiltskin calls from the other room. "Or are you still discussing?"

"You can come back," Goldie says. When he reappears, she adds, "I like your hat."

"Why, thank you!" Rumpelstiltskin says with a smile. "And I like your spunkiness."

Goldie smiles. "Thanks." She sits up straight. "Okay, Rumpelstiltskin, here's the deal. We have nothing to pay you with. But sometimes friends help each other. And Kid Bear and I would like to be your friends. And it seems like you want company. What do you think?"

"What does that mean exactly?" he asks. "You guys will hang out with me every day?"

"Sure," she says. "Or most days. You know. Sometimes I have other stuff to do."

His orange-brown eyes light up. "Okay. I want two hours every other day for at least two months. We'll make snow angels and then come inside for hot cocoa and cookies, and we'll play Monopoly and charades and hide-and-seek and sing songs."

"Great," Goldie says. "I love Monopoly. I want to be the car, though."

Rumpelstiltskin claps. "I'm the hat."

"I'm the dog!" Kid Bear says.

Prince barks.

I'm so relieved. Our plan is working! "So now we just have to find straw," I say.

"A lot of it," Rumpelstiltskin reminds me. "Good luck!"

We nod and get up.

"Thanks, Rumpelstiltskin," I say.

"Talk to you later!" Jonah adds.

"See you soon, friend," Kid Bear tells him.

"Bye for now!" Goldie says.

Rumpelstiltskin smiles and bows, and we leave.

We're back on the ledge behind the waterfall. Jonah holds his skateboard under one arm and climbs down, Kid Bear right behind him. They're on the ground before Goldie and I even start to descend. I grab Prince, and finally, we join them at the bottom. Phew. Together, we start walking in the direction of the fence.

"Where are we going to get straw?" I ask.

"Where does straw even come from?" Jonah wants to know.

"I have no idea!" I say.

"Me either," Goldie adds.

"I know!" Kid Bear exclaims.

"You know where straw comes from?" I ask.

"No," she responds. "But I know where to get a lot of it."

"Where?" Goldie and I ask at the same time.

"The mattresses in my house are made of straw," Kid Bear tells us.

"Ohhhh," Jonah says. "That's why there was that crunching sound."

"We have a big extra mattress in our closet," Kid Bear says. "But my parents won't just give it to you. They're going to want something in return. Or they're at least going to want some sort of apology gift after you, you know, ate our porridge and slept in my bed."

"That's understandable," Jonah says.

"A gift?" I say. "Hmm. All we have on us is the skateboard. And the watch . . ."

"That's really nice, but have you seen the size of my parents' wrists? That watch wouldn't fit on their pinkies. And they would crush that skateboard with one foot, too."

Jonah looks relieved. "That's good. We really need Abby's watch. And my skateboard is my favorite thing ever."

"You've only had it for a few days," I point out.

"So?" Jonah says.

"What about brownies?" I suggest. "We could bake a ton of them!" And maybe I could even bring some back for the bake sale. Sure, Robin is making them too, but I don't think she'll mind.

Goldie rolls her eyes. "Why are you guys so obsessed with brownies?"

"Because they're delicious," I say.

Kid Bear shakes her head. "Bears can't eat anything made with chocolate. Totally toxic."

Woof! Prince barks. It's the same for dogs.

"Cupcakes?" Jonah asks.

I hold my breath. Please don't tell me the fate of Goldie's father depends on my cupcake-baking skills.

"We make our own cupcakes," Kid Bear says. "But there's *one* thing my parents love, and we haven't had any in months."

I lean in. "What?"

"Honey," Kid Bear answers. "Bring them a few jars of honey and they'll definitely give you the extra mattress."

"Honey," I repeat. Great. We can probably just buy some at the grocery store in the town!

"Three jars," Kid Bear says.

Three jars for the three bears. Got it!

Then I realize something. Maybe it's not the best idea for us to go back to the bears' cottage, even with honey. They weren't exactly happy to see us last time.

"Um, Kid Bear?" I begin. "When your parents caught us in your cottage, I heard your dad say he'd teach us a lesson later. Is he going to . . ."

"Eat us?" Jonah asks.

"Eat you?" Kid Bear giggles. "Yuck." She shakes her

head. "Why do you seem to think humans are that tasty? No, my dad just meant he'd give you a lecture. He likes to lecture me whenever I do something wrong."

Jonah nods knowingly. "Our dad does, too."

I suddenly hear a roar in the distance. Uh-oh. More bears? Prince's ears perk up and he lets out a low growl.

Kid Bear's furry brown ears perk up, too. "That's my dad now, calling me home for dinner. I'd better go. See you tomorrow — with at least three jars of honey!"

We watch her run off through the forest.

"Now what?" Jonah asks.

"We find some honey, Honey," I say. "Ooh, maybe Honey can be your new nickname, Jonah."

He shakes his head. "Hard pass."

chapter eleven

Who's the Sweetest of Them All?

"Now we just have to raise enough money to buy honey from the grocery store," I say. We're still walking through the forest.

"The store doesn't have any honey now," Goldie says. "It's winter."

"So?" Jonah asks.

"There's never any honey in the winter in Bebec," Goldie explains. "Because the bees make honey, but they're hibernating now. In the spring, they'll make more and sell it to the stores and at the farmers' market. That's why the Bear family got so excited when they saw my fake note."

Great. So no honey, then. Back to square one.

"Well, what would be just as good as honey?" I ask.

Goldie rubs her lower back. "I don't know. Can we rest for a bit?" she asks. "I'm zonked from climbing up and down those rocks. Let's go sit and lean against that huge maple tree." She points across the path.

"All right," I say. We head over to the tree, Prince leading the way, and we all sit down and lean against its base. Ahh. This is pretty relaxing. Who knew maple trees were so nice to lean against?

Wait. A. Minute!

Maple tree . . .

Maple syrup!

"Jonah," I say, turning to my brother. "Didn't you just go on a field trip to the place where they make maple syrup?"

"Yup," he responds. "It was awesome. We learned how they make the syrup and got to taste it, too. Sooo good."

I nod excitedly. "Maple syrup is sweet like honey," I say. "It could be a close substitute. And it's so delicious!"

"Hey, you're right!" Jonah says.

Goldie looks from me to Jonah. "What's maple syrup?" she asks.

Jonah and I both stare at her.

"You've never had pancakes with maple syrup?" I ask.

She shakes her head. "I've had pancakes, but plain."

"Plain pancakes?" I say. "No syrup? No butter? No chocolate chips or blueberries?"

"No whipped cream?" Jonah asks, incredulous.

Goldie shakes her head. "Nope. Just plain."

I'm in shock. Even Prince cocks his head at Goldie, like he doesn't understand.

"Well, you're going to love maple syrup," I tell her.

"But how do we get maple syrup?" Goldie asks.

"From maple trees!" Jonah says.

Her eyes widen. "Really? You're kidding."

"Nope. It's true!" I insist.

"There are lots of maple trees in Bebec," Goldie says, patting the trunk behind us. "Like this one. I even have two maple trees in my backyard! Since my dad is a carpenter, he taught me a lot about different types of wood and trees."

"That's perfect," I say. "We can get the syrup from the maple trees in your backyard."

"But *how*?" Goldie asks again. "Do we have to chop the trees down? Because I can't do that."

"No . . ." Jonah says. "We stick something in the tree and then the sap comes out of the trunk. Then the sap turns into syrup. I think those are the steps."

I frown. That sounds familiar—I read about making maple syrup in a book once. "But it might be hard to make if we don't know all the steps," I say. "It's not easy, like brownies."

"Yeah. It's hard—like cupcakes," Jonah says, grinning at me.

I sigh. "Hopefully we won't mess it up as badly as I did the cupcakes." I look around the forest. The sun is setting. One thing I do know is that making maple syrup takes time. We should start in the morning. We'll need daylight to see what we're doing. If we *can* even do it.

Goldie yawns. "It's been a long day. I'm so tired."

I yawn, too.

And so does Jonah.

Even Prince yawns.

Yawns are contagious.

"You guys can sleep over at my house," Goldie says. "My dad wouldn't mind."

I glance at my watch. At least we have some time.

"Thanks," I tell Goldie. "That sounds great."

We head back through the forest and over the fence, and we cross into the town. There are so many lights on in the windows. Bebec looks beautiful.

We walk to Goldie's little stone cottage. She shows us to her dad's room. It's small, but there's a large bed with a scratchy-looking thin blanket. Prince curls up at the foot of it.

Goldie yawns again. "See you two in the morning."

"Good night," we say.

Jonah leaps onto the bed. I sit down on it. Not too hard, not too soft, but not exactly just right, either. But it's only for one night.

"I'm glad we're helping Goldie," Jonah says softly, pulling the cover up to his chin. "I feel bad for her."

"Because her dad's in jail for no good reason?" I ask.

"More that she's never had pancakes with maple syrup," he says. "Can you imagine life without maple syrup? I mean, what is the point of French toast even?"

"We'll figure out how to make it," I say.

Everything is riding on the syrup. To get the straw. To get the gold.

We have to get this right!

Just right.

chapter twelve

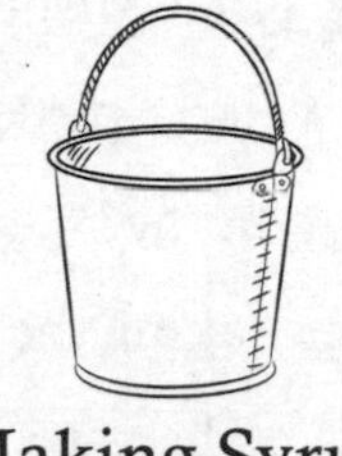

Making Syrup

Early the next morning, Jonah, Goldie, and I sit at her rickety kitchen table with Prince at our feet. Goldie serves us each a piece of banana bread.

"Did you bake this?" I ask, impressed. It looks and tastes exactly like the banana bread Rumpelstiltskin gave us.

"Sure," she says, her face turning red. She looks away. "I definitely baked it."

"OMG, did you steal this banana bread from Rumpelstiltskin's house?" I ask.

"I didn't steal it," she says. "I borrowed it."

"How did you borrow it?" Jonah asks while chewing. "Are we giving it back after we eat it?"

Goldie laughs. "No! That's disgusting."

"I saw you take a few extra pieces," I say. "I didn't realize you were taking them home."

"He was okay with me taking the pieces, so it wasn't *stealing*," Goldie explains. "Just because I didn't eat them right then doesn't change the fact that he knew what I was taking."

"Fair point," I admit. "Thank you for getting us breakfast."

She nods. "No problem."

Jonah licks the crumbs off his fingers. "Yeah, thanks, Goldie."

Woof, Prince adds.

Jonah hops off his chair. "Let's go make maple syrup!"

I can't help but feel a little worried. Are we really going to be able to make maple syrup? And what if the bears don't even want it? Then we still have no straw, and then no gold for Goldie, and then Goldie's dad can't be rescued.

Argh.

"Here's what we do," Jonah is telling Goldie. "We have

to tap into the tree bark, and then the sap comes out of the tap and pours into a bucket."

"What do you tap into the tree with?" I ask.

Jonah shrugs. "Something like a little faucet, I think."

Goldie's face brightens. "A spigot? My dad used them when he built sinks for his carpentry business."

"Yeah, a spigot!" Jonah responds.

"We can look in my dad's tool supplies," Goldie says. "In the shed out back. I sold just about everything. But there are some odds and ends left."

We go outside and make our way toward the small brown shed in Goldie's yard. The weather is a little warmer than yesterday, and sunny. Goldie's backyard is tiny, but it does have plenty of trees. Prince runs around, sniffing at the ground and barking happily. He waits for us as we go inside the shed.

There are only a few small dented tools piled on the floor. We spot a bucket right away, and Jonah picks it up. It's rusty on the outside, but large. "Perfect," I say. "Now we need the spigot."

Goldie and Jonah sort through a pile of tools, and finally

Goldie holds up something small and metal. "I think this is it!" she cries.

One end has a spike that could go into the tree trunk. And the other end has a tube where the tree sap could spill right into the bucket.

"Yes, that looks like what they used on the field trip," Jonah says. "Let's try it!"

We hurry back out into Goldie's backyard, and Goldie leads us over to the two maple trees.

I pick up the metal tap and try to stick it into one of the trees. "It won't go in!"

"Let me try," Jonah says. He attempts to stab it in. "The tree is too hard!"

"Are any trees soft?" I wonder.

"I think we need a hammer," Goldie says, "but I sold off all my dad's."

Crumbs. I look down, worried that this is a dead end for us. Then I notice Prince pawing at some rocks on the ground. Rocks!

"Can we use this?" I ask, picking up one of the biggest ones.

Goldie bangs the rock against the tree . . . and it works! She's able to stick in the spigot. But . . .

"I think it's upside down," I say. "The faucet part should be pointing toward the ground so the sap goes into the bucket, maybe?"

Goldie twists the spigot and now it's the way it's supposed to be. I think.

"Now we put the bucket underneath and wait," Jonah says.

"Okay," Goldie says, hanging up the bucket.

La, la, la.

I peer into the bucket. Empty.

"Guess it'll be a while longer," I say.

We wait.

And wait.

"Look!" Goldie exclaims, pointing at the tap.

We all look. A white, watery substance is pouring into the bucket. Just a little. But still!

"Is that maple syrup?" Goldie asks.

"It's sap," I explain. But I forget the steps you have to take to turn the sap into syrup. Why am I so bad with recipes?

"Next we take the bucket of sap and pour it into a pot," Jonah says. "Then we cook it!"

"And then it becomes maple syrup?" Goldie asks.

"Yep," I say. I remember now, too. He's right!

Goldie walks over to the bucket and sniffs it. "Smells a little sweet."

"Good," I say. "Sour maple syrup would be gross."

We wait some more and peer in the bucket again. It's about a quarter filled up.

We hang out in Goldie's yard, playing catch with Prince. Goldie runs over to check the bucket every five minutes.

"A watched pot never boils," I tell her.

She frowns. "Of course it does. That makes no sense. Why wouldn't a watched pot boil? Unless your eyes have cooling powers?"

"It's just an expression," I say. "My nana likes to use it. But point taken."

Goldie continues to check it every five minutes, until finally she yells, "The bucket is full!"

And it is! We carry the bucket into Goldie's kitchen. There's a big pot on the stove. Goldie pours the sap into the pot and then turns on the burner.

"We're not allowed to use the stove at home without asking our parents," Jonah says.

"My dad lets me use the stove," Goldie says. "I'm in charge of the cooking, actually," she adds proudly. She looks at the pot. "So how do you know when it's done?"

"I think it'll be ready when the sap turns dark brown and gets thicker," Jonah says.

"Are you sure?" I ask. "Because this needs to be perfect. Too much is at stake."

"I hope so," Jonah says.

We wait. A watched pot never boils, so we sit at the kitchen table. The syrup cooks pretty fast and the kitchen fills with steam. I open the window to air it out. Then I go over to the stove. The syrup is ready! I think. For all that sap, there is only a small amount of syrup in the pot. But it's all we've got. I turn off the burner and let the syrup cool for a minute.

My heart speeds up as I dip in a spoon and give it a taste.

OMG. "It's pretty good!" I exclaim. "Really!"

Goldie dips a spoon in and tries it. Her green eyes widen. "Wow, not bad!"

"It *is* good," Jonah says, tasting from his own spoon.

"But . . . is it just right?" I ask. "It needs to be just right. Not too sweet, not too tart . . ."

"I don't care if it's just right," Goldie says. "I don't even know what just right is supposed to taste like. Honestly, in this case, good enough is fine with me."

Fair point.

Sometimes good enough is good enough.

Hmm. I wonder if the cupcakes I made were good enough, too. Was I being too hard on myself? No. What was I going to sell? Chunks of cake? I shake my head.

I pour the syrup into four small empty bottles I find on the counter. We only need three bottles, but if something happens to one of them, I want an extra.

Plus, I *could* always take the bottle back with me and sell maple syrup at the bake sale.

Goldie tucks the four bottles into a sturdy bag.

Time to go back to the bears.

chapter thirteen

Snow Cone

To save time, we decide to ride Jonah's skateboard to the bears' cottage. Well, Jonah really decides because I still don't think it's a safe idea. But at least we won't be going downhill. Somehow, we all pile onto the skateboard — Jonah, me, Prince, and Goldie, plus the bag of maple syrup bottles — and ZOOM through the town.

When we reach the bears' cottage, we come to a stop. The Bear family is outside in their yard, painting. Mother Bear, Father Bear, and Kid Bear have three easels set up with canvases on them. They're all wearing smocks and painting beautiful pictures of the forest. If I weren't still a little scared of the bears — well, the parents — it would be an adorable scene.

"Hi!" I call out, my voice shaking.

"Yay!" Kid Bear says. "Mom, Dad, my new friends are here! And look, they have a skateboard. I really want a skateboard," she tells us.

Father Bear turns around, his brown eyes narrowed. "Friends with people. Will wonders never cease?" he asks. He clears his throat. "Human children, I need to tell you that —"

I feel a lecture coming on. "That we should never have broken into your house," I interrupt, "eaten your porridge, sat in your chairs, or slept in your bed. You are absolutely right. We are so, so, so sorry."

There's a pause.

"You sat in our chairs?" the dad asks.

Oops.

"Yes," I say.

"But we didn't break them!" Jonah calls out.

"We're glad to hear that," Mother Bear says. She clears

her throat and pushes up her glasses. "Our daughter told us about your apology gift and the trade you'd like to make. If you have the jugs of honey, we'll give you our extra straw mattress."

Yes!

I pull one of the bottles of maple syrup out of the bag and hold it up. "There are two more in here for you," I say.

Father Bear stares at the bottle in my hand. "That looks awfully dark for honey."

"That's because it's not honey," Jonah reports.

Mother Bear frowns. "The deal was for honey!"

"I did say honey," Kid Bear adds, looking at us with big, brown, disappointed eyes. "I was really looking forward to having some on my porridge this morning."

"This" — I say, stepping closer with the bottle — "is maple syrup. It's sooo delicious! You can put it on pancakes or French toast. Or even porridge!"

"We don't want that maple . . . thing!" Father Bear growls. "We want honey!"

"Honey, honey!" Kid Bear chants.

This isn't going the way I thought it would.

Goldie takes the bottle and holds it out toward the bears. "But just take one sniff at how good it smells. Mmmm," she says, inhaling. "So sweet!"

"I said no!" Mother Bear growls.

Goldie's face crumples, and her hands shake. Some of the syrup spills onto a pile of snow that the bears must have shoveled off the walkway.

Everything's a mess.

Woof! Prince licks some of the maple-y snow. *Woof-woof.* His tail is wagging.

"Prince likes it!" Kid Bear exclaims.

"Oh, yeah, maple syrup is good on snow," I say. "It's a maple snow cone."

"Can I try?" Jonah asks me.

"Sure," I say. "The snow looks pretty clean."

Jonah reaches down, grabs a chunk of maple-drizzled snow, and tastes it. "Now this is good."

Kid Bear grabs a chunk of maple snow and pops it in her mouth. "Yum!" she announces. "This is amazing. Like ice cream! Mom, Dad, I bet it would be great on my porridge."

I guess the mess is a tasty mess?

Mother Bear steps forward and takes the bottle from

Goldie. She sniffs it. "Well, that does smell good." She hands the bottle to Father Bear.

He also sniffs it. "I must say that it does."

"Okay," Mother Bear says. "We'll try it on our porridge. If we like it, you can have the mattress. You can come in, but please try not to eat any of our food or take a nap in our beds. Or break any of our chairs." She raises an eyebrow.

A totally fair ask, considering.

We go inside. There are three bowls of porridge cooling on the table. I hold Prince in my arms, just to be on the safe side.

Mother Bear pours some maple syrup in each bowl and stirs each one with a spoon. "Okay, come and get it."

The bears sit down at the table and place their napkins on their laps. For bears, they have excellent table manners.

Father Bear blows on his porridge. He dips his spoon in and brings it to his mouth.

I hold my breath.

Please like it!

Father Bear's brown eyes widen. "This is absolutely delicious!"

Mother Bear eats a spoonful. "So tasty!"

Kid Bear gobbles up her porridge. "Maple syrup for the win."

Phew! Jonah, Goldie, and I exchange relieved grins. It worked!

Father Bear stands up. "Okay, you have a deal. We will trade you the straw mattress for the maple syrup."

"Yay!" Kid Bear says.

Goldie's face melts in relief. "Thank you!"

Father Bear disappears into the bedroom and returns with a straw mattress.

We did it!

Goldie accepts the mattress from Father Bear and thanks him again.

Father Bear sits back down, and the Bear family continues eating.

"Um, Abby?" Jonah asks.

"Yeah?" I say.

"How are we going to lug that mattress through the forest and up the rocks?" he asks.

Good question.

I look at my watch. It's already after 5:00 A.M. in Smithville.

We only have about eight Bebec hours left. And we still have no gold.

Too bad we *can't* skateboard up a cliff.

"This mattress is really hard to carry," I say when we get outside with it.

I'm holding one end, and Goldie is holding the other. Jonah is standing between us, holding up the middle, with his skateboard under one arm. Prince is trotting along, looking like he wishes he could help.

"Let's get it on top of our heads and we'll walk single file through the forest till we get to the cliff," Jonah says.

"Or . . ." I look at the skateboard. "We put the mattress on the skateboard and push it!"

Yup. That's much easier.

"How will we get it up the cliff, though?" Goldie asks.

Another good question.

We hurry as fast as we can, pushing the mattress on the skateboard. Finally, we reach the frozen waterfall.

"Now what?" Goldie asks, looking up at the rocks.

We decide that Jonah will climb the rocks while Goldie, Prince, and I slide the mattress across the frozen lake and then hoist it up to him.

As Jonah starts his climb, I take a careful step onto the lake. This probably isn't a great idea. But it seems sturdy?

Goldie glides onto the ice and twirls. "Whee! This is fun!"

She's right. We slide the mattress across the lake. Prince pushes the skateboard across with his little nose. He's so helpful!

When we get to the frozen waterfall, we lift the mattress up and up and up . . . and Jonah grabs on to the other end. He manages to maneuver the mattress onto the ledge. Hurrah!

But now Goldie and I have to climb up the rocks ourselves. Sigh.

First, Goldie and I watch from below as Jonah knocks on Rumpelstiltskin's door.

The little window slides open and Rumpelstiltskin's orange-brown eyes peer out. Then the window closes, and I hear him unlocking all his locks.

"Hello," he says to Jonah. Then he looks down at me and Goldie, standing on the lake. "I should probably invest in a ladder for guests," he adds with a shrug. "Next time."

"Where's Rapunzel's hair when we need it?" I grumble as Goldie and I start to climb up the rocks.

"Who?" Rumpelstiltskin and Goldie ask at the same time.

"No one," I say. I guess the fairy tale characters really don't know each other. Except for Goldie and Rumpelstiltskin, of course.

Goldie, Prince, and I carefully climb up the rest of the way. Whew! We help Jonah push the mattress inside Rumpelstiltskin's house, and gather inside the living room.

"What now?" I ask.

"Now you need to pull the straw out of the mattress," Rumpelstiltskin says.

We find a zipper, open it, and all kneel and start grabbing out fistfuls of straw.

"Abby, you have straw in your hair!" Jonah says with a giggle.

"You have straw on your nose!" I tell him.

Finally, all the straw is in a pile on the floor.

"How are you going to spin the straw into gold?" I ask Rumpelstiltskin.

Rumpelstiltskin raises an eyebrow and shakes his head. "I don't share my secrets!" he tells us. "Now step back! I need room."

We step back.

And wait.

Rumpelstiltskin walks over to the straw. He stares at it. Then he does a strange little dance, kicking up his legs. He then picks up the straw with his arms and spins around fifteen times. Wow! He is actually spinning the straw.

The straw disappears in a puff of yellow smoke! I can barely see anything — the smoke is in my nose and my mouth and, ouch, in my eyes.

I cough and blink, and then I see it:

A pile of gold coins in his arms.

Seriously. Gold coins.

OMG. He did it!

"Rumpy, you are a rock star!" Jonah says.

"Do not call me Rumpy," he snaps. "That's a terrible nickname. It does not sound dignified at all."

I give Jonah a look.

"Sorry," Jonah says. "And thank you so much!"

"No problem," he says. He dumps the coins on the floor, turns away, and sits on his big blue velvet couch. I want to ask him what's wrong, but we don't have much time. Goldie needs to get to the palace to free her dad, and Jonah and I need to get back to Smithville.

"Fill your pockets with the coins," Goldie says.

Jonah, Goldie, and I grab palmfuls of coins and put them in our pockets. Prince helps by nudging more coins into our hands. When we're all done, we stand up, our pockets heavy and bulging.

"Wait!" Rumpelstiltskin shouts.

Uh-oh. Here it is. Is he going to demand something else?

"Yes?" I ask cautiously.

"I see Kid Bear isn't with you," Rumpelstiltskin says. "I guess she changed her mind about being friends."

"No," Goldie says. "She's just eating porridge with her parents right now."

Rumpelstiltskin brightens. "Oh. So the friendship is still on? Even though you now have your gold?" He bites his lip. He looks worried.

Aww.

Goldie smiles. "Of course it is. I'm excited to make snow angels and have hot chocolate. And all those other fun things you mentioned. We'll visit you tomorrow afternoon."

Rumpelstiltskin claps. "I'm so happy!"

Me too. Who would have thought that Goldilocks, one of the three bears, and Rumpelstiltskin would end up being BFFs?

"You guys can make friendship necklaces!" I suggest. "Look at mine." I show them the beaded one I'm wearing that says FRAP — Frankie, Robin, Abby, Penny. Maybe they can be RKBG — Rumpelstiltskin, Kid Bear, Goldie? Hmm. They could use a vowel in there.

"Fun!" Rumpelstiltskin says.

"Another time," Goldie says. "When we're not rushing to save my dad."

Right.

We hurry back outside.

"Good luck," Rumpelstiltskin says. "You'll need it."

Then he closes the door.

We have the hundred gold coins the king asked for. Hopefully we won't need luck.

chapter fourteen

To the Palace

We hop over the fence into town and ride Jonah's skateboard-sled over to the palace, zooming as fast as we can.

Up close, the palace is eerie but beautiful. It's also the biggest castle I've ever seen. It goes on and up forever with pointy towers and turrets.

We jump off our skateboard-sled. Then we hurry across the long plank over the moat and up to the gate. A guard dressed in black with gold stitching is standing in front of it.

"What is your business with the king of Bebec?" he demands.

"We're here to pay a fine to free a prisoner," Goldie says.

The guard takes a walkie-talkie out of his pocket, then turns and mumbles something into it.

"The king will be out shortly," he announces.

Goldie is practically jumping up and down with nerves and excitement.

In a few minutes, the king appears in the arched doorway. He's tall, over six feet, burly, and about my parents' age. His eyes are small and beady. He's wearing a yellow-gold crown, a yellow-gold robe, yellow-gold flip-flops, and three yellow-gold necklaces. It's a lot of gold. He's very shiny. I wish I was wearing sunglasses.

"I am King Ned, ruler of the kingdom of Bebec!" he bellows. "Who is this prisoner you've come to free?"

"Hello, King Ned," Goldie says. "I'm Goldie and I'm here to pay the fee to free my father, Clinton, from your prison."

"Oh," the king says with a sneer. "You must mean Clumsy Clinton."

Goldie's cheeks turn red. "My father isn't clumsy! He broke that statue by accident."

The king leans his head close to Goldie. "If I say he's clumsy, he's clumsy!" he shouts.

Goldie's cheeks get redder and I can practically see steam coming out of her ears like in a cartoon.

"Well," King Ned says. "Where is my bag of gold?"

We all pull gold coins from our pockets and hold out our hands to the king.

"Count the coins, guard!" the king demands.

The guard walks up to me. He takes my coins, one by one, from my hands and drops them into a velvet pouch. "One, two, three . . ."

This is going to take a while.

The guard moves on to Jonah and counts his coins. "Twenty-six, twenty-seven . . ."

Oh, brother.

Now it's Goldie's turn. She holds out her full palms.

"Ninety-nine, one hundred," the guard says, and drops the last two coins into the full pouch.

"Where's the rest?" King Ned asks with a frown.

"The rest?" I repeat.

"Yeah, you said a bag of gold coins," Goldie says. "Everyone in Bebec knows that means one hundred coins."

The king lifts his chin and looks down his long, thin nose at Goldie. "It does. But you owe me interest for the two weeks Clumsy Clinton has been in my jail. Fourteen more coins. One for every day he's been there."

I gasp. "That's not fair!"

Goldie looks like she might cry. "We don't have fourteen more coins."

"Buh-bye, then," the king says.

"That's not right!" Jonah shouts. "You can't say one thing and then another!"

The king laughs. "Oh, yes, I can. Because I'm the king."

I can't believe it. *No!*

He turns to leave. I see Goldie's shoulders shaking. She's crying!

King Ned is the worst, meanest, most horrible king ever! He has a ton of gold. He doesn't need more.

I have to do something.

But what?

What do I have to offer?

Oh!

"Maple syrup!" I call out.

The king stops and turns. "Excuse me?"

I still have one bottle of maple syrup left in the bag.

"Oh, King Ned," I say. "We have something better than

fourteen gold coins in this bag." I hold it up. "Yes! It's better than gold. It's *liquid* gold. It's sweet and delicious. And no person in Bebec has ever tried it before."

His beady eyes widen. "What is it?"

I put the bag down and take out the last bottle of maple syrup. "Only the most amazing thing you will ever have on pancakes or French toast!"

"Or porridge," Jonah adds. "Or snow. If you wanted to eat snow."

"Why would anyone want to eat snow?" the king asks with a scowl, but he steps closer. "Let me see that."

I hand him the bottle.

He pulls off the cap and sniffs. "Mmm. That smells amazing!"

Goldie looks at me with hope in her eyes.

"What did you say this is called?" he asks.

"Maple syrup," Goldie says. She bites her lip.

"Spoon!" the king bellows.

Another guard rushes over with a spoon. A gold spoon, obviously.

The king pours out a spoonful. He puts it into his mouth.

His eyes close. He's smiling!

"Oh my word," King Ned says. "This is good. Absolutely incredible. I must have some on my afternoon snack, my evening meal, and my breakfast!"

Yes! Jonah and I high-five each other.

Even Prince gives a little woof.

Goldie looks very relieved.

The king pours himself another spoonful. "How do you make this?" he asks Goldie.

"It's a special recipe," Goldie says. "Very complicated and time-consuming. It would take hours just to tell you."

"Wow!" King Ned exclaims. "Isn't that something?" He looks at the bottle. "It *is* liquid gold! I might change the name to that. Liquid gold."

He steps closer to us. He sure is tall. And imposing.

"You, you, you, and you," King Ned says, pointing at me, Goldie, Jonah, and Prince. "I command you all to make enough maple syrup to last the royal family one year. I will free Goldie's father after you deliver the syrup."

Um, no. Jonah, Prince, and I have to get home. I look down at my watch. It's already 6:00 A.M. in Smithville. We have five more hours here left. Tops. Definitely not enough time to make enough syrup for a year!

"What?" Goldie cries. "You can't do that! It'll take forever to make that much syrup!"

Prince barks forlornly.

"Then I suggest you get started now," the king says.

"Achoo!"

The king stops and turns. "Who dared sneeze while I was talking?"

A guard steps forward. He's trembling!

"Um, I did, King Sir."

"Take him to jail immediately," King Ned orders the other guards. "Put him in cell eleven. Next to Clumsy Clinton."

"My dad is not clumsy!" Goldie snaps.

I catch the guards grimacing as they take Sneezy away.

"Now where was I?" King Ned says. "Oh, yes. The liquid gold. You will make me a year's worth right now!"

Ugh. I was hoping he forgot that.

"But we can't make any more syrup," I say. "There just isn't time. Jonah and Prince and I have to get home!"

"Home?" the king repeats. "Where is home? Don't tell me you live in the forest with the animals. Although *he* belongs in Montario," he adds, glaring at Prince.

"We live in Smithville," I say, and feel a pang of homesickness. "It's far away."

The king lifts his chin again. "I command you to stay," he orders. "I hereby declare that you are all the official liquid gold makers for the royal family."

"No!" I say.

"Yeah," Jonah says. "No!"

"No one dares tell ME no." King Ned turns to guards lining the side of the palace doors. "Guards! Seize them! Throw them into cell number twelve with Clumsy Clinton."

The guards grab us. Nooo!

Woof! Prince lunges for a guard's ankle.

The guard yells, "Get that mutt!"

But Prince is too fast for them. He runs away, and no one can catch him. Go, Prince! I watch worriedly as he scurries off out of sight. I hope he'll be okay, but I know Prince is tough. He'll wait for me and Jonah somewhere outside the palace as long as he needs to.

"We'll catch you, you ugly mutt!" the guard yells.

"He's not ugly. He's adorable!" I insist.

The guards push us around to the side of the palace,

where there's a row of twenty doors. It looks sort of like a motel. But it's not a motel. It's the palace jail!

"This is your cell!" one of the guards announces when we reach a door marked NUMBER 12. He opens the door and shoves us all inside.

The cell is tiny. There's a small window on the door and another even smaller one in the back of the room. A man with curly golden hair is sitting on a bench, his head hanging down. He looks so sad.

"Dad!" Goldie cries.

The man looks up. His green eyes widen and he jumps to his feet. He rushes over to us. "Goldie!"

"No one defies the king!" the guard says from outside. He slams the door and locks it.

I sigh. This isn't good.

Goldie and her dad are hugging. "I've missed you so much, Dad!" she cries.

"I've missed you too, sweetheart," her father says.

Aww.

At least Goldie and her dad are back together again.

Mission, um, accomplished?

chapter fifteen

Trapped

This is not my first time in fairy tale jail.

And what I've learned is this: There is always a way out.

Usually.

Except here, I don't see one.

Yet.

Goldie and her dad are sitting on the bench, happy to be together again. Goldie introduces us to him and explains that we tried to help her free him.

Goldie's dad stands up and shakes my hand and then

Jonah's. "I'm Clinton, Goldie's father. Thank you for helping my daughter. I really appreciate it."

"Not sure you should thank us if it didn't work," Jonah says, his shoulders slumping.

Clinton shakes his head. "You did your best. King Ned is a horrible person. He puts people in jail for the smallest wrongdoing. One prisoner has been here for a month because he was eating an apple and crunched too loudly."

"King Ned is the worst," I say.

And we know from bad kings.

"I don't know why Queen Paula puts up with him," Clinton says.

The miller's daughter. Maybe she's terrified he's going to lock her up again.

I look at the two small windows in the cell. They both have black bars on them. I wobble the bars to see if they're loose. Nope.

"Trust me," Clinton says. "I've tried. Those bars aren't budging."

Crumbs.

I glance at my watch. We only have one Smithville

hour to get home in time. If we're not back at seven, when our parents come into our rooms to wake us up, they are going to freak out. Understandably.

I pace back and forth.

"Abby?" Jonah asks. "Where do you think Prince is?"

Good question. I don't know. But we could use his help.

A few hours later, I'm still trying to think of a way out. I can see a little bit of sky through the window at the back of the room — and it's getting dark now.

Creeeeeak.

We all turn. The door to the cell opens. A guard is holding a tray.

"Dinner is served," he says, and puts the tray on the floor. The heavy door closes behind him and I can hear a lock turn again. I hate the sound of that lock.

"Dinner? What time is it?" Just as I ask the question, five chimes ring out from the clock tower in town.

I look at my watch. It's 6:36 A.M. at home. Not good.

"Ooh, I'm starving," Jonah says. "What did they bring? I am kind of in the mood for sushi."

I look on the tray. There are four crackers and four tiny pieces of cheese and four small cups of water.

"That does not look like a California roll," I say.

"In King Ned's prison," Clinton says, "that's dinner."

We all munch quietly on our crackers. As quietly as you can munch on crackers, that is.

Woof!

I sigh. I must be hearing things because I thought that was Prince barking. And he's definitely not here.

"Abby! Look!" Jonah cries. He's pointing out the little window. "It's Prince!"

We all rush over to the window. Suddenly, I see a face appear. A furry face, with brown eyes and a black nose. But it's not Prince.

"It's Father Bear!" I whisper.

Mother Bear appears beside him, and I see that Kid Bear and Prince are behind her. "Your dog came to find us," Mother Bear explains. "We don't speak dog, but he barked and barked and we had a feeling you were in trouble."

"We followed him over the fence and all the way here," Kid Bear says.

"Good job, Prince!" Jonah says, giving a little fist pump.

"Prince is such a good boy!" Goldie says. Aww. Prince is starting to grow on her.

Woof! Prince agrees.

"You're going to help us escape?" I ask the bears.

"Of course," Father Bear says. "You introduced us to maple syrup. So we owe you."

I smile. "Hurrah!"

Father Bear grips the bars and tries to move them. "They're too strong," he says.

"Oh, no!" Mother Bear cries. "We have to get them out."

But how?

"Do I have to do *everything*?" another voice says.

I know that voice!

Rumpelstiltskin appears outside the window. He's wearing his blue velvet suit and his high hat.

"How did you know we were here?" I ask.

"I told you — I don't share my secrets," he says, and winks.

"Yay, Rumpelstiltskin!" Jonah says.

I grin. "Can you help us get out of here?"

"Duh! Of course I can!" he says. "Step aside, animals."

But then I notice Rumpelstiltskin's eyes get wide. He

seems to be watching something I can't see from the jail cell. What? What's going on?

Suddenly, I hear a familiar sound. But I can't place it. I turn toward the front door. Where do I know that annoying sound from? It's like a grating, screechy noise.

Wait. Someone's riding on Jonah's skateboard! I squint through the window in the door. It's Kid Bear!

She comes barreling toward our cell. I thought Jonah was fast on that thing? Kid Bear is going *super* fast!

"Whee!" she exclaims, putting her arms to the sides for better balance.

The edge of the skateboard crashes into the cell door — and it flings open!

"We're free!" Clinton cries.

"Wow," Goldie says. "No magic required." She gives Kid Bear a high five.

"We're so proud of you!" I hear her parents exclaim from outside the other window.

"That was *awesome*!" Jonah says. "You're even better on the skateboard than I am."

Kid Bear's chest puffs out.

"I was wondering where I left it," Jonah adds.

"It was just outside the palace," Kid Bear says. "Great idea!"

"Um, sure," Jonah says sheepishly. "That was totally on purpose."

"Thank you so much!" I tell Kid Bear.

"Aw, it was nothing," she responds. She turns to her parents. "Maybe you'll buy me my own skateboard now?" she asks hopefully. She slides the skateboard over to Jonah, who stops it with his foot.

"We'll see," Father Bear says from outside the window.

Rumpelstiltskin frowns. "I would have gotten you guys out, though."

"We appreciate magical *and* nonmagical help," I say.

I glance out the open door. I can see the guards over by the front of the palace, talking. I hear one complain about how mean King Ned is. The king put the guard's grandmother in prison yesterday for looking *old*.

I shake my head. King Ned doesn't deserve to run this kingdom. I think about the sign on the fence. *Kingdom of Bebec. Welcome to all who deserve to live here.* The kingdom should be for *all* residents.

I turn to the bears. "Now what?" I ask.

"We'll distract the guards," Mother Bear says. "So you can run. Run all the way to our cottage, and we'll meet you there."

"Aren't you afraid to help us?" I ask. "King Ned will put you all in jail if he catches you."

"We're not afraid of that meanie," Mother Bear says. "Besides, he doesn't care enough about the animals to put us in jail. He doesn't even consider us his subjects."

"You'll be safe in our cottage," Father Bear says. "The king and his guards don't go into the forest."

"Ready?" Mother Bear asks once Kid Bear has joined her parents outside. "Let's go!"

She, Father Bear, and Kid Bear turn and run toward the guards, roaring REALLY loudly.

It works! The guards are busy running away from the bears and don't notice as Jonah, Goldie, her dad, and I all dash out of the cell and away from the palace. Rumpelstiltskin and Prince join us and we all keep running.

We hop over the fence, run into the forest, ride Jonah's skateboard straight to the bears' cottage, and rush inside.

Deep breath. Deep breath. I look at my watch: 6:42. My parents' alarm goes off in three minutes!

"How about a little something to eat?" Father Bear

asks once he arrives back with Mother Bear and Kid Bear. "Dinner before you go? I made mac and cheese."

"Um . . . sure," I say as my stomach growls. But then we really have to run. We're out of time.

"Should we stand?" Jonah asks, since there are only three chairs at the table.

"Please sit," Mother Bear says, and adds, "I have some folding chairs in the closet."

She pulls out enough chairs for all of us, as Father Bear puts on oven mitts and takes out his pan of mac and cheese. "Does maple syrup go with this?" he asks.

"Definitely not," Jonah says. "Mac and cheese should only be eaten with ketchup."

"What's ketchup?" Goldie asks.

OMG.

"You don't have ketchup?" Jonah cries, his eyes almost popping out of his head. "You have to learn how to make ketchup. Abby, we have to teach them how to make ketchup! Before we go! We have to!"

"I don't know how. Do you? I'm guessing with tomatoes?" I take a quick look at my watch. "But Jonah, we don't have time to make ketchup! Or eat mac and cheese. We only have a few minutes to get back to Smithville!"

At least we know where the portal is — the bears' mailbox.

Suddenly, we hear footsteps. Lots and lots of footsteps.

"What's that?" I ask.

We all rush to the window.

It's King Ned's army! And leading them is King Ned on a huge *ostrich*.

"Bear family," the king bellows. "Surrender the prisoners! We want Rumpelstiltskin, too! I've been trying to capture that magical little man for years."

"Don't hand over Rumpelstiltskin," Jonah insists. "He was nice to us!"

"We won't. He's a friend," Goldie adds with a firm nod.

"Yeah!" Kid Bear says.

Rumpelstiltskin puts his hand on his chest, his orange-brown eyes misty as he looks around the table at us. "That's the nicest thing anyone's ever said about me."

Father Bear jumps out of his chair, opens the window, and growls. "We refuse!" he calls out to the king.

Mother Bear roars. "That's right!"

Prince barks.

"You can't refuse!" the king shouts. "No one dares defy me! I am the king of Bebec!"

"Someone get me a mattress!" Rumpelstiltskin whispers to the rest of us inside the cottage.

Huh?

"A mattress? Why?" Goldie's dad asks, looking confused.

"Just trust me!" Rumpelstiltskin says, and I do.

So do the bears, it seems. Mother Bear and Kid Bear run into the other room and return with a mattress.

Is Rumpy going to turn the mattress into gold and pay the king to go away?

They drop the mattress at Rumpelstiltskin's feet.

"Thank you," he says. He grabs a fork from the table, rips open the mattress, and starts to pull out heaps of the straw. When his arms are full of straw, he opens the door.

"What are you doing?" Mother Bear cries.

"I got this," Rumpelstiltskin says, with a crooked smile. He steps outside.

"Seize them!" the king yells to his guards.

"Nope," Rumpelstiltskin orders. "With the exception of

Goldie and her father, we are not even your royal subjects. Therefore you don't tell me, or the Bear family, what to do."

"Oh, yes, I do! Seize them!" King Ned yells again.

"Again, nope," Rumpelstiltskin says. "Anyway, you want some gold?" he asks the king. "You know I'm the one who makes the gold."

The king's eyes widen. He nods.

"Hold the straw with me," Rumpelstiltskin says. He takes the king's hands. The straw is piled on top of their arms. Then he does his little dance.

"Now spin!" he yells.

They hold hands and spin, around and around, fifteen times.

And right before our eyes, the straw sprouts into pillars. Gold pillars.

Rumpelstiltskin lets go of the king's hands, takes a step back, and . . . the king is trapped. Between the gold pillars. He's in a gold jail cell.

Oh, wow.

Yes!

"But how is that possible?" Clinton asks, gaping at Rumpelstiltskin.

Rumpelstiltskin smiles. "I can do more than just coins."

"Oooooh, gold," King Ned says, caressing one of the bars. "But release me immediately!"

"Nope," Rumpelstiltskin says. "Look, I said it again!"

"Why, you little —" the king begins to shout.

"What is happening here?" we hear a woman's voice call out.

We turn around to see a woman riding an ostrich toward the cottage.

"It's the queen!" Kid Bear exclaims. Then she curtsies.

The queen is beautiful. She has brown skin and long brown hair twisted into a braided bun below her crown. She's wearing a silky orange gown and bright purple snow boots. But uh-oh — are we in trouble with *her* now?

"Get me out of here, Paula," the king orders from his gold cell.

The queen smiles. "Sorry, dear. You are where you belong."

Wait, what?

The king turns red and starts stomping his feet. He's screaming and yelling inside his golden cage.

"Silence!" Queen Paula insists. "I will take over running the kingdom now."

She turns to Rumpelstiltskin.

"Rumpelstiltskin," the queen continues, "a very long time ago, we made four deals. You honored them all. You turned my straw into gold. And you let me keep my beloved baby because I was able to tell you your name. That baby is all grown up and in college in a faraway land, but one day she'll be queen."

Rumpelstiltskin looks worried. "And?"

"And I trust you. Sure, you tried to steal my kid, but you never lied to me. Would you consider being my advisor?"

He thinks for a moment, then shakes his head. "I'm afraid not, Queen Paula. I prefer not to be at anyone's beck and call. I'd rather do my own thing and hang out with my friends." He smiles at Kid Bear and Goldie before turning back to the queen. "But thank you for the offer."

The queen laughs. "Thank you for locking up my evil husband." She touches her royal scepter to the top of his head. "You are now officially a knight of the kingdom. You are hereby known as Sir Rumpelstiltskin."

"Cool!" Rumpelstiltskin exclaims.

The queen clears her throat. "I declare that all the prisoners — except for King Ned — in our jails are now free. Each former prisoner will be awarded a bag of gold upon release. Guards, go free them and hand out the gold."

"Yes!" Goldie says. She turns to her father. "Now you'll have enough money to buy back all your carpentry tools. We'll be able to build new furniture. And eat three meals a day again!"

Clinton and Goldie hug.

The queen smiles and reaches into the backpack on her ostrich and pulls out a bag of gold. She hands it to Clinton. "I'm sorry for how you were treated," she says.

"Hey!" the former king pouts.

"Guards," she says, ignoring him, "bring the king back to the palace. I know just the cell he'll stay in." Then she turns to me and Jonah and the Bear family. "Children, thank you for everything," she goes on. "Mr. Bear, Mrs. Bear, and . . . what's your name, little one?"

"Andrea!" Kid Bear says.

Oh! A vowel! Her name starts with a vowel. Their friendship necklace can say GAR! Or RAG? Or GRA!

"Andrea, and Mr. and Mrs. Bear — you have been

amazing protectors of our people. We will take down the fence, and all parts of Bebec can be united!"

Everyone claps. Hurrah! Andrea Bear gives us all high fives.

"Thank you," Father Bear says.

"Good day," the queen says. "Let's go," she says, turning to her ostrich.

"Copy that," says the ostrich.

Wow. Every animal really does talk here! Poor Prince.

The queen climbs back on her ostrich and the other ostrich follows. The guards follow them, carrying the gold jail and its screaming prisoner high in the air.

Rumpelstiltskin turns to us. "Well, I guess this is good-bye. Oh, and kids? You can tell people to call me *Sir* Rumpelstiltskin now. How's that for a nickname?"

I grin. "That works. Bye!"

Sir Rumpelstiltskin smiles, snaps his fingers, and disappears into thin air.

No wonder he doesn't mind his rocks and scary ledge door. He doesn't have to use it.

"I wish I could snap my fingers and make myself disappear," Jonah says. "I also wish I could ride a talking ostrich."

Of course he does. "Maybe in another story." I look at my watch. Ahhh! It's seven! I turn to Goldie, her father, and the Bear family. "We have to go!" I tell them. "It was great to meet you all!" I throw my arms around the bears to say good-bye. They hug me back. They are warm, soft, and very, very furry. Not scary at all.

Then Goldie throws her arms around *me*. She smells sweet. Like maple syrup.

"Thank you for helping me," she says. "You and Jonah and Prince. I didn't think I had any friends, and it turns out I had three. Then I made two more — Rumpelstiltskin and Andrea."

"I'm glad you trusted us," I say.

"I'm glad you trusted *me*," she says, pulling back. "I know I was a mess when you met me. But you still thought I was worth helping."

"Of course you were worth helping," I say. "And messy isn't bad."

"Very true," she says, flipping a curl off her shoulder.

Very true, I think.

"Abby, look!" Jonah says.

I look where he's pointing. The bears' mailbox is purple and swirling.

I dare to look at my watch. It's 7:02 at home. We're so late!

AHHH!

I swallow. This is bad.

"Now we REALLY have to go!" I say to everyone.

"Bye!" they all call back.

Jonah grabs his skateboard, and he, Prince, and I rush to the mailbox.

We jump right into the swirling purple mist.

I have no idea what's going to happen when we land back home. *If* we land back home. What if the broken mirror sends us somewhere else?

I cross my fingers and hope for the best.

We land in our basement. Jonah and I pop up off the floor. He's still carrying his skateboard. Prince wags his tail. Phew. The mirror still works!

I hear my parents upstairs calling us.

"Where *are* they?" my dad says. "It looks like they slept in their beds."

"Should we call the police?" I hear my mom ask.

"Uh-oh," I say.

What are we going to tell them?

I think. And think. And think some more. But I have no clue!

"Abby, we're going to be in big trouble with Mom and Dad," Jonah says.

"Probably," I agree.

"Should we tell them the truth?" he asks, his eyes wide. "Again?"

We tried to tell them once, but then Maryrose erased their memories.

"Maryrose?" I call, turning back to the mirror. "What do you want us to do?"

But there's no answer. I glance at the crack in the mirror — oh, no.

It's longer than it was before. Almost a foot now.

"Maryrose, are you still in there?" I call.

Silence.

I have a bad feeling about this.

All I hear is my mom calling my name. My dad calling Jonah's name.

We have to get upstairs. But where is Maryrose?

chapter sixteen

Nice to Meet You

We rush upstairs to the main level just as my parents are coming downstairs from the bedrooms.

"There you two are!" my mom says in a flustered voice.

"We took Prince for a walk," I say.

I glance at Prince. He lets out a little woof and wags his tail.

It's not a lie, exactly. We *did* take Prince for a walk. Through the mirror and into two stories in one.

My dad clears his throat. "When you leave without telling us —"

A lecture is starting.

"We acted very irresponsibly," I jump in. "We made you worry for no reason. We absolutely should have told you, or at least written a note. We are so, so, so sorry."

Pause. Dad looks at Mom.

She nods.

"Well, next time, let us know," she says.

"Sorry," I say. "We will. Promise!"

"Got some skateboarding in before school, huh?" my mom asks Jonah.

Jonah grins. "The mountain was awesome!"

"Mountain?" my dad repeats. "There are no mountains in our neighborhood."

I stare at Jonah. He stares back.

"A sidewalk is kind of a tiny mountain," he says.

My dad smiles quizzically. "Okay, buddy. You better come eat something before school."

Woof! Prince barks.

"You can have a doggie biscuit, Prince," my mom says, then heads into the kitchen with my dad.

"Wow," I say to Jonah. "Everything's okay."

Jonah and I go into the kitchen.

"Abby, what are you doing with those . . . um . . . cupcakes?" Mom says.

I see the messed-up cupcakes still on the counter. Oops.

"They're not perfect," I say. "But maybe I can still do something with them."

"Like what?" Jonah asks.

"Like . . . cake pops!" I say.

"Oh!" Jonah exclaims. "Smart."

"You don't have that much time," my dad says.

"I'll do them fast," I say. I wash my hands and then start smushing the cupcakes into balls.

"I'll help," Jonah says. "I'll get Popsicle sticks. Oh! And I know exactly what the missing ingredient for your icing is."

"Cake pops?"

"Hah. No! Maple syrup!"

Oooh. "But we don't have time to make maple syrup," I say.

"Why would you make maple syrup?" my mom asks. "We have some in the fridge."

I laugh. "Right."

Jonah takes the jug out of the fridge and places it beside me on the counter. "Liquid gold," he says.

I smile and pour some in the bowl.

My cake pops turn out great. Messy, yeah. But maybe messy is okay. Maybe there is no such thing as *just right*. Maybe not perfect can still be delicious. Maybe it's okay to have a hairline crack or two. Maybe a crack allows you to try something you never would have expected. Like two stories in one.

When my maple cake pops are all packed up, I run upstairs to grab my backpack for school. I go into my room and notice my jewelry box on my dresser. My nana gave it to me. It's decorated with all the fairy tale characters on it. But every time I go into a story, the characters change to reflect what happened in the story. And how we messed it up.

I turn the box around and then I see her — Goldie! She, her dad, Paula the queen, Rumpelstiltskin, and the three bears are sitting at a fancy table in a grand dining room. It must be at the palace. Maybe the queen had them over for brunch. And OMG — Goldie, Rumpelstiltskin, Andrea the bear, and Queen Paula are all wearing necklaces. And they say GRAP in gold letters! Hah!

They're all eating big bowls of porridge, and a beautiful jug of maple syrup sits in the middle of the table.

The jug says, GOLDIE'S SYRUP.

Oh! Hurrah! I guess she started her own business after all.

I take off my watch to put it into my jewelry box.

But when I open the lid, a purple mist swirls out.

I gasp.

What's going on?

Suddenly, right in front of me, the purple mist grows and grows and starts to take shape.

It turns into a young woman. She's a little taller than I am, and she has a long face and wavy dark hair. I've seen her before. In the mirror.

OMG. It's Maryrose!

She's standing right in front of me.

"Ahhh!" I cry. I can't help it.

She gives me a gentle smile. I can't tell what color her

eyes or hair or skin are. She's sort of . . . see-through. She looks very real and like she's not there at all. Both at the same time!

She is a fairy, after all.

"Maryrose! What were you doing in my jewelry box?" I manage to squeak out.

"I'm hiding in there," she explains. "Just for a while. Till I figure things out."

"What things?" I ask. "What's wrong?"

"The crack in the mirror let me escape."

My mouth drops open. "No way."

"Abby!" my dad calls from downstairs. "Time to leave for school!"

Maryrose smiles again. "Go ahead, Abby."

"But where are you going to go?" I ask her, my head spinning.

"I'll be fine. We'll talk more when you get back. I need your help with something."

I can barely believe that *Maryrose is in my room*. Hiding out in my jewelry box. And that I'll soon know everything.

I want to stay and talk NOW. But I can't without making my parents suspicious.

"We're going to help you," I tell Maryrose. "As soon as I come home."

Maryrose nods and turns back into purple mist. I run down the stairs and out the door, counting the seconds until I get home again.

Don't miss Abby and Jonah's next adventure,
where they fall into the tale of *The Twelve Dancing Princesses*!

Look for:
Whatever After #15: **JUST DANCE**

acknowledgments

A bag of gold to:

The Scholastic team: Aimee Friedman, Taylan Salvati, Lauren Donovan, Rachel Feld, Erin Berger, Olivia Valcarce, Melissa Schirmer, Elizabeth Parisi, Abby McAden, David Levithan, Lizette Serrano, Emily Heddleson, Robin Hoffman, Sue Flynn, and everyone in Sales and in the School Channels. My amazing agents, Laura Dail and Samantha Fabien, Austin Denesuk, Matthew Snyder, and Berni Barta, and queen of publicity, Deb Shapiro. Rachel and Terry Winter! Extra extra thanks to Lauren Walters. And thanks to Shannon Messenger for sparking the idea for the book's twist!

All my friends, family, writing buddies, and first readers: Bonnie Altro, Elissa Ambrose, Robert Ambrose, the Bilermans, Max Brallier, Julie Buxbaum, Jess Braun, Rose Brock, Jeremy Cammy, Julia DeVillers, Elizabeth Eulberg, Stuart Gibbs, Karina Yan Glaser, Brooke Hecker, Emily Jenkins, Gordon Korman, Leslie Margolis, the Mittlemans, Aviva Mlynowski, Larry Mlynowski, Zibby Owens,

Lauren Myracle, James Ponti, Melissa Posten, Melissa Senate, Courtney Sheinmel, Jennifer E. Smith, Christina Soontornvat, the Steins, the Swidlers, Louisa Weiss, and the Wolfes.

Extra love to Chloe, Anabelle, and Todd.

Hugs and wishes to my Whatever After readers. You are just right.

Read all the **Whatever After** books!

Whatever After #1:
FAIREST of ALL

In their first adventure, Abby and Jonah wind up in thc story of Snow White. But when they stop Snow from eating the poisoned apple, they realize they've messed up the whole story! Can they fix it — and still find Snow her happy ending?

Whatever After #2:
IF the SHOE FITS

This time, Abby and Jonah find themselves in Cinderella's story. When Cinderella breaks her foot, the glass slipper won't fit! With a little bit of magic, quick thinking, and luck, can Abby and her brother save the day?

Whatever After #3:
SINK or SWIM

Abby and Jonah are pulled into the tale of the Little Mermaid — a story with an ending that is *not* happy. So Abby and Jonah mess it up on purpose! Can they convince the mermaid to keep her tail before it's too late?

Whatever After #4: DREAM ON

Abby and Jonah are lost in Sleeping Beauty's story, along with Abby's friend Robin. Before they know it, Sleeping Beauty is wide awake and Robin is fast asleep. How will Abby and Jonah make things right?

Whatever After #5: BAD HAIR DAY

When Abby and Jonah fall into Rapunzel's story, they mess everything up by giving Rapunzel a haircut! Can they untangle this fairy tale disaster in time?

Whatever After #6: COLD as ICE

When their dog, Prince, runs through the mirror, Abby and Jonah have no choice but to follow him into the story of the Snow Queen. It's a winter wonderland . . . but the Snow Queen is mean, and she FREEZES Prince! Can Abby and Jonah save their dog . . . and themselves?

Whatever After #7: BEAUTY QUEEN

Abby and Jonah fall into the story of *Beauty and the Beast*. When Jonah is the one taken prisoner instead of Beauty, Abby has to find a way to fix this fairy tale . . . before things get pretty ugly!

Whatever After #8: ONCE upon a FROG

When Abby and Jonah fall into the story of *The Frog Prince*, they realize the princess is so rude they don't even *want* her help! But will they be able to figure out how to turn the frog back into a prince all by themselves?

Whatever After #9: GENIE in a BOTTLE

The mirror has dropped Abby and Jonah into the story of *Aladdin*! But when things go wrong with the genie, the siblings have to escape an enchanted cave, learn to fly a magic carpet, and figure out WHAT to wish for . . . so they can help Aladdin and get back home!

Whatever After #10:
SUGAR and SPICE

When Abby and Jonah fall into *Hansel and Gretel*, they can't wa
to see the witch's cake house (yum). But they didn't count on th
witch trapping them there! Can they escape and make it back t
home sweet home?

Whatever After #11:
TWO PEAS in a POD

When Abby lands in *The Princess and the Pea*—and has troubl
falling asleep on a giant stack of mattresses—everyone in th
kingdom thinks SHE is the princess they've all been waiting fo
Though Abby loves the royal treatment, she and Jonah need t
find a real princess to rule the kingdom . . . and get back hom
in time!

Whatever After #12:
SEEING RED

My, what big trouble we're in! When Abby and Jonah fall int
Little Red Riding Hood, they're determined to save Little Red an
her grandma from being eaten by the big, bad wolf. But there
quite a surprise in store when the siblings arrive at Little Red
grandma's house.

Whatever After #13: SPILL the BEANS

Abby and Jonah FINALLY land in the story of *Jack and the Beanstalk*! But when they end up with the magic beans, can they get Jack out of his gigantic troubles?

Whatever After Special edition #1: ABBY in WONDERLAND

In this Special Edition, Abby and three of her friends fall down a rabbit hole into *Alice's Adventures in Wonderland*! They meet the Mad Hatter, the caterpillar, and Alice herself . . . but only solving a riddle from the Cheshire Cat can help them escape the terrible Queen of Hearts. Includes magical games and an interview with the author!

Whatever After Special edition #2: ABBY in OZ

Abby's not in Smithville anymore! In this extra-enchanting second Special Edition, Abby and her friends are off on a new adventure inside *The Wonderful Wizard of Oz*. Can they find the courage, brains, and heart — along with a whole cast of new friends — and make their way back home? Includes bonus games and activities.

about the author

Sarah Mlynowski is the *New York Times* and *USA Today* bestselling author of the Whatever After series, the Magic in Manhattan series, and a bunch of other books for teens, tweens, and grown-ups, including the Upside-Down Magic series, which she cowrites with Lauren Myracle and Emily Jenkins, and which was adapted into a movie for the Disney Channel. Originally from Montreal, Sarah now lives in Los Angeles with her family. Visit Sarah online at sarahm.com and find her on Instagram, Facebook, and Twitter at @sarahmlynowski.

Fill my Cup, Lord

A Teatime Devotional

Emilie Barnes

with Anne Christian Buchanan

FILL MY CUP, LORD

Eugene, Oregon 97402

Library of Congress Cataloging-in-Publication Data
Barnes, Emilie.
MFill my cup, Lord / Emilie Barnes with Anne Christian Buchanan.
MMp. cm.
M1. Bible. O.T. Psalms XXIII—Meditations. 2. Christian life—Meditations. I. Title.
BS1450 23rd.B37 1996
242—dc20 95-46904
CIP

Printed in the United States of America.
96 97 98 99 00 01 02 - 10 9 8 7 6 5 4 3 2 1

To my daughter, Jenny, our Princess #1
Without you, my sweet one,
this book would have never been written.
I love you deeply and dearly.

Contents

A Word for Thirsty Souls

The Lord is my shepherd; I shall not want.

Psalm 23:1

How can so many people's lives be so full and their hearts and souls be so thirsty?

That's what I find myself wondering as the years go racing by me.

At church, at our seminars, even in restaurants or airports I meet men and women whose schedules are packed, who are pouring all their energy into keeping up with their lives and soon find themselves all poured out. Physically and emotionally and spiritually, they are desperately in need of a refill.

And of course, I run on empty, too, at times. My tasks as a writer and speaker, as a wife and mother and grandmother and friend, pull at me until I feel parched and drained.

That's when I find special meaning in that wonderful old song I heard for the first time so many years ago as a young Jewish girl who had recently come to know the Lord.

"Fill my cup, Lord," the singer sang that evening. That was long before I began my collection of lovely china teacups. It was before my children came, before my mother died, before my writing and speaking ministry was even a gleam of possibility. And yet something deep in my spirit echoed the cry of that song.

Today, knowing a lot more about teacups and even more about the ways that life can drain us, I find that "Fill my cup" is a constant cry of my thirsty heart.

Sometimes, during especially trying times, I feel like Oliver Twist standing there with his tiny, polished bowl, pleading with hungry eyes, "Please, Sir, I want some more."

Those are times when I am at the end of my rope, when I know I have no means of nourishing myself and am willing to risk humiliation to beg for the life I need. At those times my gracious Lord Jesus, so unlike the selfish beadle in Dickens' story, pours out his presence with an especially generous hand.

More often, though, I find myself holding up a cup that is not quite empty, a heart not quite that humble and hungry. Sometimes my cup holds the old, cold residues of rancid ideas or moldy attitudes or leftover values and stubborn pain. I still need the Lord to fill my cup, but first I need to have it emptied and rinsed clean. That requires both my willingness and the Lord's grace.

Something else about the cup I hold up for the Lord's filling: it's cracked and flawed, the gleam of the porcelain marred with imperfections. I need to remember that no matter what my polish or glaze, I am still an earthen vessel. And sometimes I feel as patched and glued as the one cup I was able to rescue after a shelf in my armoire came crashing down. Perhaps that's why I seem to empty out so easily. I leak, so I need refilling on a daily or even an hourly basis.

"Fill my cup, Lord."

I hope that's your heartcry, too, as you open this book.

I imagine you sitting there quietly, perhaps with a cup of fragrant tea at your elbow and this book in your lap. Perhaps you have managed to carve out a tiny minute of respite from ringing phones and crying children. Or perhaps your days are lonely and too long, and you've taken this minute as a way of structuring the empty hours.

Whatever your circumstances, you, too, can hold up your cup and it will be filled.

If your cup is polished and dry, hold it out for the Lord's plentiful pouring.

If your cup is full of the old and the unsatisfying, hold it up for the Lord's cleansing.

If your cup is cracked and broken, hold it up anyway, for the Lord's resources are plentiful and can keep even leaky cups replenished.

Come to him as you are, cup in hand, and hold it up to receive his blessings.

And then you will say, as I have said over and over again in wonder and amazement—

"Surely . . . my cup runneth over."

Fill my cup, Lord . . .

I offer you my cup of stress

that you may fill it

with quietness.

1

A Cup of Quietness

He makes me to lie down in green pastures;
He leads me beside the still waters.
Psalm 23:2

Quiet time.

It's a lovely phrase, isn't it? To me, "quiet time" summons up images of stillness and serenity, of a quiet communion with God on a beautiful garden patio or a cozy window seat—reading his Word and praying and journaling while a fragrant cup of tea steams at my elbow.

And I have had wonderful quiet times like that.

But these days, I have to confess, my quiet times are not always so quiet—at least not at first. Sometimes they start out more like silent wrestling matches as I struggle with my fears, my worries, my pain.

Do you have times like that? Times when you seek out solitude, flee into stillness, only to find that your worries have followed and refuse to leave you alone? Or times when your schedule is so demanding that quiet time with God feels like just one more chore you can't manage?

If so, I have good news for you.

A quiet spirit is not a requirement for a quiet time with the Lord.

Yes, I need to be willing to come to him, to offer him my cup filled with whatever is troubling me. But if I do that, I have found that he can supply the quiet spirit. If I can manage to hand over that cup of trouble, he can and will fill it to overflowing with serenity and peace.

What a wonderful thing to know, to remember, to remind yourself of when you feel overwhelmed with busyness or with pain. You don't have to come to him quiet. You just need to come to him.

The last few years have not been easy ones for our family. Not only has our schedule been packed with important but wearying obligations, but the trauma of an impending divorce has also torn a big rip in the fabric of our lives. I've had to watch as people I love make decisions I don't understand or approve of, and I've agonized as others I love suffer hurts I can't soothe. I've had to wait for answers and understanding and resolution that just haven't come yet.

That's why so many of my quiet times lately have started out anything but quiet. Often I have been angry or torn or worried or scared.

But that's why I need the quiet in the first place. When my mind is full of clamor and my cup is full of trouble, that's when I most need to hear God's still small voice, and to feel his peace.

This is what I'm learning once again as I hold up my cup to the Lord and seek to spend time with him:

My quiet time is not a gift I give to God.

My quiet time is a gift God gives to me.

I don't offer him my quiet time. I simply offer him my time, my self. He's the one who provides the quiet spirit.

I come to him with my cup of confusion and worry. He's the one who takes that cup and empties it and then pours it full of quietness and peace.

He supplies the quiet. I supply the time.

That's one reason I can have quiet time, if necessary, in places that are not absolutely quiet. Quiet doesn't always require solitude. In fact, I've had some of my most meaningful quiet times on airplanes or in crowded restaurants, with engine noise buffeting my ears and people pressed in around me. My spirit was with the Lord, silently holding up my cup to him, and he provided the gift of quietness in the midst of a whirlwind.

But quietness does seem to require that I make the conscious effort to get away from the distractions of those who need me or who claim my attention. That's why I can have quiet time on a noisy airplane where no one knows me but not during a family dinner or on the floor of a conference where I am speaking. I need to pull away, to shut a door, to put space between me and the ordinary demands of my day. And in order for that to happen, I usually need to schedule my time for being with God.

But I don't need to "get quiet" in order to draw near to God. I just need to be willing to come to him.

Of course, it's wonderful to go to a place where physical quietness can help foster spiritual quietness. God has always spoken quieting words to me through his creation, so I love to have my quiet times out of doors. I love to go to a park, into a yard, under a tree—where I can see the butterfly flap its wings in spring or watch the colored leaves drift off the trees in fall. God works in my heart through nature, soothing my spirit with growing things and gentle breezes.

For several years now, my quiet times have tended to coincide with my morning walks. Yes, I love a quiet moment with a cup of tea, but I prefer company for tea. And yes, I have my daily times with my prayer notebook, when I try to be faithful to my prayer promises, interceding for my family and for my church and for those who have requested my prayers.

But when my cup is full of trouble and I really need to be alone with God, I like to lace up my tennies and set out on the path along the long irrigation canal that runs through our town.

I know that two-mile course now like the back of my hand. I know where the rocks jut up, where the path grows narrow, where the orange blossoms smell the sweetest, where a recent rain will make a mud puddle on the path. I feel safe among the many other joggers and walkers (and their dogs) that use the path. And somehow the rhythm of my Reeboks on that familiar path helps me walk my thoughts toward my heavenly Father.

Because I know the route so well, I sometimes read as I walk—or read a bit and then walk a bit. I carry a little book of scriptural prayers, and I read a few and then let them work into my mind as I stride along. Over the past year or so, I've prayed through several of these books more than once (I write the date in the back cover when I finish one and start over).

But I don't wait until I feel spiritual to start walking. I simply put one foot in front of the other. As I walk I simply let my thoughts and feelings and confusions and stresses rise up in my mind, turning them over to God. And most of the time, by the time my forty-five-minute walk is over, the quiet has usually come.

Sometimes it takes awhile. Most days, in fact, it takes at least twenty minutes for the noise and busyness of my everyday life to sift out of my head and for my internal strife to settle down. It seems to take that twenty minutes of walking to get my cup rinsed out and ready for the Lord's filling.

I may not be consciously praying or even thinking during that time. I'm simply walking and letting the breeze wash over me and listening to the birds sing and smelling the orange blossoms and letting the Scriptures or whatever else I've been reading speak to my spirit in the silence.

And then, in the last twenty minutes of my walk, something almost always happens. The "to dos" and "I've gottas" and "but what abouts" in my head begin to subside, and God's peace begins to settle into my spirit. And then, when I'm finally able to listen, God whispers his word of peace and comfort, or guidance and challenge.

Sometimes I remember a passage of Scripture. Sometimes a knotty problem seems to unravel itself in my head. Sometimes I am simply strengthened to go on with my life. Tears often flow—tears of relief and release as my cup of troubles is poured out and the quietness flows in to take its place.

No, it doesn't always take that long. I have found that if I offer to God whatever time I have, he honors that time. If I only have fifteen minutes but bring those fifteen minutes to him, he can give me what I need in those fifteen minutes. But, then the sweet taste of his peace leaves me wanting more and more.

And no, it doesn't happen every single time. It's not a cut-and-dried transaction: I come to God; he gives me peace. It's a relationship. The peace comes from spending time with the one who speaks in silence. The quietness comes from being with him and letting him rearrange my thought processes.

There have been a few times on the canal path (and on the patio and on the airplane) when nothing seems to change—when I have come to God agitated and gone away agitated. Sometimes in retrospect I can understand what happened. I was holding on too tightly to my troubles, unwilling to give up control even to God. Or I needed to learn something or do some growing, and God was using my discomfort to motivate me. I don't know all the answers for those times when my quiet time never got quiet. God rarely works on my schedule, and sometimes my cup filled with peace more slowly than I expected.

But I have to tell you that those times have been rare, even in the difficult years. Almost always, I have come away from my quiet times with my cup overflowing. Again and again, when I gave the Lord my chaos, he has given me his peace.

More and more, that is what I am yearning to do.

The longer I live, the more I thirst for those quiet times in my heavenly Father's presence, the more I long to climb up into the lap of my Abba-Daddy and enjoy the security of those everlasting arms. Sometimes I feel like a toddler stretching my own arms up, dancing on my toes, begging to be held by the One who loves me so much.

"Up, Daddy. Want up."

And then he lifts me up.

The longer I live, the more I know that if I will just hold up my cup to him, even my cup of anger and stress and trouble and confusion, he will be faithful to fill my cup with the peace of his presence.

Savoring God's Word . . .
A Sip of Quietness

When He gives quietness, who then can make trouble?

Job 34:29

I wait for the Lord, my soul waits,
And in His word I do hope.

Psalm 130:5

My soul, wait silently for God alone,
For my expectation is from Him.

Psalm 62:5

Better is a handful with quietness
Than both hands full, together with toil
and grasping for the wind.

Ecclesiastes 4:6

In returning and rest you shall be saved;
in quietness and confidence shall be your strength.

Isaiah 30:15

Peace I leave with you, My peace I give to you; not as the world gives do I give to you. Let not your heart be troubled, neither let it be afraid.

John 14:27

For God is not the author of confusion but of peace.

I Corinthians 14:33

Be anxious for nothing, but in everything by prayer and supplication, with thanksgiving, let your requests be made known to God; and the peace of God, which surpasses all understanding, will guard your hearts and minds through Christ Jesus.

Philippians 4:6-7

Come to Me, all you who labor and are heavy laden, and I will give you rest. Take My yoke upon you and learn from Me, for I am gentle and lowly in heart, and you will find rest for your souls. For My yoke is easy and My burden is light.

Matthew 11:28

Now to Him who is able to do exceedingly abundantly above all that we ask or think, according to the power that works in us, to Him be glory.

Ephesians 3:20-21

Fill my cup, Lord . . .

I offer you my cup of criticism

that you may fill it

with encouragement.

2

A Cup of Encouragement

He restores my soul.

Psalm 23:3

"What a beautiful reception," I thought as I flipped through the recently developed stack of photographs.

There was my newly married niece, her face flushed with happiness. There was her new husband, beaming and proud. There were the children, dressed up and excited, and the older ladies beaming with satisfaction at another wedding in the family.

And there I was in my white Battenburg lace dress—looking pretty good, if I did say so myself!

I should have looked good. I had poured a lot of effort into pulling myself together perfectly for the occasion, paying special attention to my hair, my hose, my shoes, my bag. Trying so hard to get everything just exactly right so that my elderly auntie, for once, would have nothing to criticize.

Well, I finally did it, I thought as I flipped another picture. There was my aunt sitting at her table with a big smile on her face. My smile was big, too, as I remembered it. For the first time in my memory, she hadn't said a single critical word about how I was dressed or how my makeup looked or anything else. I'd talked to her on the phone several times since then, and she still hadn't made a negative comment.

I glanced at the clock. I really needed to call her again. She was very independent, even in her eighties, but I still tried to check on her every day or two.

Auntie was in a wonderful mood when she answered the phone. She had gotten her pictures, too. So we reminisced about the ceremony, speculated on how the new couple would get along, and replayed the events of the reception.

"And, oh, Emilie," she enthused, "you looked just beautiful."

By now I was actually grinning. This was almost too good to be true.

And then she added in a thoughtful voice, "Emilie . . . you really need to consider getting a padded bra."

Zing. I could feel my grin slipping down to the floor, that old familiar knot tightening my stomach.

I should have seen it coming, of course. It was only the hundred-millionth time she had done that to me. (I was beginning to realize that she did it with everyone she loved.) But that didn't keep the words from stinging—as they always stung. With one little remark, my auntie had managed once more to fill my cup with criticism.

Do you know somebody like that, who seems to delight in pouring doses of criticism? If you don't, just wait a little bit, and one will almost certainly come knocking at your door. Your critic may even be ringing your doorbell or calling you on the phone right now. Someone you just can't please. Someone who excels in bowling over your confidence with just a word or a look.

It may be direct, overt, controlling:

"You shouldn't pick up the baby when he cries."

"I'm afraid blue just isn't your color."

"Thank you, but it's just not our style. I know you won't mind if I return it."

Or it may be more subtle—a backhanded compliment or just a calculating sniff and a martyred look:

"You're so patient. If my children acted like that I'd be mortified."

"Well, yes, I suppose so . . ."

But no matter how the criticism is poured, the message is clear. You did it wrong. Your efforts just don't measure up. You just aren't good enough . . . smart enough . . . pretty enough.

It's so hard to live freely and creatively and lovingly with that kind of criticism. It's hard to risk flying high when you're always afraid of being shot down. I know, because my critical auntie had been pouring out caustic cupfuls for me ever since I could remember.

It wasn't that she didn't care about me. In fact, she had always made it clear that I was special to her. But my auntie's critical spirit led her to express her love with constant attempts to control and change me. From the time I was small, nothing about me had ever been quite right for her—my hair, my speech, my manners, my clothes, my children, or anything else.

And how did I respond?

For years, I just tried harder.

I spent so much of my life in a constant struggle to live up to my aunt's impossible standards.

I would visit the hairdresser and have my nails done before a visit. She would give me the number of *her* hairdresser and manicurist.

I would scour the stores for just the right birthday gift. She would return it.

I would choose my words and my grammar with care, trying so hard not to say anything wrong. She would still find something to criticize.

And then it finally hit me.

All my life I had been holding out my cup to my auntie, waiting for her to fill it with encouragement and praise. And she couldn't do it! Her own cup was too full of a critical spirit to pour anything different into mine. Holding up a bigger or better or more beautiful cup wasn't going to make any difference. And Satan was still using her poured-out criticism to make me feel inadequate and insecure and thus damage my ability to share Christ's love.

If I wanted my cup to hold anything other than criticism, I needed to stop holding it out to my auntie so trustingly. When she poured the criticism in anyway—as she was bound to do—I needed to take what I could learn from her critical words and then dump the bitter brew down the drain.

But it wasn't enough just to empty my cup. If I did, my aunt or someone else would fill it up again. What I needed to do was to keep my cup filled with love and acceptance and affirmation and encouragement from a dependable Source. I had to decide who I wanted to listen to—who was going to have power over me. And making that decision is what would enable me to empty out the criticism, wash out the cup, and then get it refilled from God's bubbling bounty of encouragement.

That, gradually, was what I learned to do. But it didn't happen all at once. It took a lot of time and practice and prayer. That particular painful afternoon, God and I had already been working on this process of emptying and filling for several years.

What did I do in response to her criticism?

I thanked my aunt for the idea. (I hadn't worn a padded bra since high school.) Then I pictured myself slowly turning over that cup of criticism and pouring it out, wiping it clean, holding it up again. And I prayed, *Please, Lord, fill my cup with your love. Let me respond to her criticism with gentleness. Even though she fills my cup with criticism, let me fill her cup with encouragement.*

And, please, Lord, I added *don't ever let me act like that to others. Teach me to see and express only what is good and healthy in my friends and family.*

How often, I wonder, have I filled others' cups with my criticism by stressing the negative and not focusing on the positive? Whether I liked it or not, I was trained by an expert to look at others with a critical eye. And when your cup is full of criticism, it's so easy to let it overflow into the cups of those around you! That's another reason it's so important that I keep emptying the cup of criticism and filling it with positive things—so I can fill others' cups with encouragement instead of criticism.

First Peter 3:4 reminds us of the importance of cultivating the "inner self, the unfading beauty of a gentle and quiet spirit, which is of great worth in God's sight" (NIV). That's what I want for my life—a cup of encouragement and affirmation rather than a cup of criticism.

Yet even as I write this, I realize I may have fallen into being critical toward my critical aunt! Yes, she had her faults. But I truly believe she did the best she could with what she was given. And she had so many good qualities. She gave generously to those in need and to many who were not in need. She modeled hard work, rigorous honesty, and the nurturing of family connections. (Until she died, she regularly sent money to our extended family in Romania.) She left me so much—not only her material possessions, but also a heritage of helping others. As I empty my cup of criticism, I want to fill it with encouragement and affirmation and also with gratitude for this woman who loved me and shaped me.

There is so much about any person that is good and beautiful. So focusing on the positive doesn't mean being naive or unrealistic or blind. It simply means learning to accept myself and others for what we are—human beings with faults and good points and also the capacity to grow.

It also means I'm learning to accept the fact that I'm not the one in charge of the universe. It's not my job to change everybody or even to enlighten the world about its problems! Besides, criticism hardly ever changes anybody—except to make the criticized person more angry, resentful, stubborn, and, perhaps, critical of others.

Now, I am not saying we should never speak with one another about problems. I am not saying we should blind ourselves to faults or ignore difficulties. I am not saying we should always sit on our opinions and bite our tongues. And I am certainly not saying we should never return gifts or give our honest opinion about how someone's hair looks.

There is a difference between honest discussion and hurtful accusation. There is a difference between being aware of someone's faults and shattering that person's confidence. There is a big difference between tactfully returning a gift or stating an opinion and filling someone's cup with criticism.

But discerning that difference may involve some honest self-evaluation. A critical spirit can be easy to rationalize, especially in the name of honesty or helpfulness. When there's doubt, I truly believe it's better not to say anything.

So, is your cup filled with criticism?

Are you holding onto your cup and filling the cups of others with the bitter brew?

If you think that's possible, I urge you to stop and pour out your cup of criticism before it poisons you and the people you love. Then begin the work of cleaning out the hurts in your life that make you critical of others.

When criticism starts to fill your cup again, and it will, recognize it for what it is and stop letting it in. Instead, make a point of pouring beauty and love into your cup and the cups of others. Look for something to admire in yourself and others and make a point of expressing that admiration.

If that's hard, think again. We are all children of God, created by him. He made us each beautiful in his sight. Make the effort to find that beauty in yourself and others.

I'm not saying it's easy—the habit of criticism can be deeply ingrained. My auntie remained critical of me until the day she died, and I'm sure I have moments when the old poisonous brew drips from my cup into someone else's.

But the cycle of criticism really can be broken. This is how it works:

First, you examine your cup. You take a tiny sip to see if there's something there you need—some truth you need to hear, even in that unpleasant form. Then you turn your cup, dump out that poisonous draft, and hold out your cup to be filled with God's love and acceptance and encouragement.

And you do it again, repeating the process whenever the criticism begins to flow. Better yet, you keep your cup so full of good things that there's no room for the biting, critical words.

You can do that, you know, because the Lord is always there for you, waiting to fill your cup with encouragement and affirmation, waiting mercifully to restore your soul when it has been shriveled by criticism. He does it through the words of Scripture, through the soft whisper of his Holy Spirit, and especially through the people who love and accept and support you.

Surely I wouldn't have been able to cope with my auntie's criticism if there hadn't been people who kept my cup brimming with encouragement and affirmation. But God has filled my cup generously through these special people in my life.

I think of my mother, who always believed in me and excelled at the gentle art of teaching without criticizing.

Or I think of my husband, Bob, whose ongoing affirmation has lifted me higher than I ever imagined, and my children and grandchildren, who encourage me in a hundred ways.

Mentors such as Florence Littauer lovingly badgered me into becoming a speaker and a writer when I had no idea I had anything to say or any gift for saying it.

My special friends, who know me so well and love me anyway, give me daily encouragement to keep on.

And I am profoundly grateful to all the hundreds of women who read my books and attend my seminars and then call or write to let me know that God has touched their lives through me.

If God, who knows me more intimately than even Bob or my mother, can use me as a channel of his blessings—and make no mistake, he uses you, too!—then how can I let my cup remain full of criticism? How can I not be encouraged when I remember that God has not only accepted me, but wants to use me to do his work in the world?

That is not to say that everything about me is acceptable to God! In fact, the Scriptures make it clear that I am always falling short of the mark. I never get it all right, no matter how hard I try. No one does.

But here's the amazing lesson for those of us whose cup of criticism has too often been full.

God himself, when confronted with the enormity of human sin, didn't respond by criticizing us. He didn't sit up there in heaven and harp about the way we humans manage to mess up every good thing he ever made.

What he did was become a human being and live among us.

And there's more.

Of all the people on earth, there has been only One with the right and the power to criticize any other human. There has only been One without sin, one person worthy to throw stones at others. And he didn't do it.

What he did was die for us. And that fact alone is enough to fill my cup to overflowing.

But there's more to the story about my critical auntie.

Less than three years after my niece's wedding reception, this same aunt lay dying in her hospital bed. She was eighty-eight. She had fought death to the end with the same determination she had brought to the rest of her life. But now she was very tired, and we knew the end was near.

I remember the last evening in particular. Darkness had already fallen by the time I arrived at the hospital, and the soft lighting in my auntie's room contrasted with the harsh lights of the corridor.

"Your auntie has been very peaceful today," the woman in the next bed told me in her soft Jamaican accent. She was a very sick woman herself, going blind with diabetes. We had gotten to know her a little during the past few days.

I looked at my auntie. Maybe she did look peaceful, compared to her hard days of fighting. But she was so clammy and thin and the color had gone from her and her breathing was so heavy. And as I sat there beside her I began to think back over the years, about the time she had spent with me and the gifts she had given me and also about all the pain she had brought to my life. Somehow it all seemed minor now.

So I put my arms around my auntie, and I put my hankie to her brow, and I began to recite the Twenty-third Psalm, "The Lord is my shepherd, I shall not want. . . ."

And then the soft voice from the next bed was joining in, reciting with me. "He maketh me to lie down in green pastures; he leadeth me beside the still waters. He restoreth my soul. . . ."

In the silence of the bare room that sweet Jamaican woman and I recited the familiar words of the psalm. We finished, and then we recited it again, and it was as if angels were hovering in the room.

And now, I thought, my aunt really did look peaceful—or perhaps the peace was in my heart. I pulled the covers up and I tucked her in, and I left. That was the last time I was able to look into my auntie's face, her eyes, and hold her hand, because she died a very few moments after that.

I later found out that the woman in the next bed, a brilliant woman who spoke five languages, had learned the Twenty-third Psalm as a little girl and recited it every night before she went to sleep. What a blessing she was to me in those difficult hours. How she filled my cup with encouragement!

I truly do not know where my auntie is now. Unlike my mother, who came to know Jesus in her later years, my Jewish auntie died without acknowledging the Messiah.

But I do know that the last words she heard were God's Word, and her last human contact was a loving embrace. And I know that happened only because I, by God's grace, had learned to empty out my cup of criticism. God's great and amazing mercy to me during that difficult time was the gift of powerful acceptance and prayer for this woman who had hurt me so deeply, but who also loved me much. And, oh, how that beautiful gift helped to restore my soul.

Savoring God's Word . . .
A Sip of Encouragement

Do not withhold good from those to whom it is due, when it is in the power of your hand to do so.

Proverbs 3:27

There were some who were indignant among themselves, and said, "Why was this fragrant oil wasted? For it might have been sold for more than three hundred denarii and given to the poor." And they criticized her sharply. But Jesus said, "Let her alone. Why do you trouble her? She has done a good work for Me."

Mark 14:4-6

Judge not, and you shall not be judged. Condemn not, and you shall not be condemned. Forgive, and you will be forgiven.

Luke 6:37

For God did not send His Son into the world to condemn the world, but that the world through Him might be saved.

John 3:17

There is therefore now no condemnation to those who are in Christ Jesus, who do not walk according to the flesh, but according to the Spirit.

Romans 8:1

Whatever things are true, whatever things are noble, whatever things are just, whatever things are pure, whatever things are lovely, whatever things are of good report, if there is any virtue and if there is anything praiseworthy—meditate on these things.

Philippians 4:8

Encourage the timid, help the weak, be patient with everyone. Make sure that nobody pays back wrong for wrong, but always try to be kind to each other and to everyone else.

1 Thessalonians 5:14,15 (NIV)

Do not speak evil of one another. . . . He who speaks evil of a brother and judges his brother, speaks evil of the law and judges the law. But if you judge the law, you are not a doer of the law but a judge.

James 4:11

And above all things have fervent love for one another, for "love will cover a multitude of sins."

1 Peter 4:8

Fill my cup, Lord . . .

I offer you my cup of resentment

that you may fill it

with forgiveness.

3

A Cup of Forgiveness

. . . He leads me in the paths of righteousness for his name's sake.
Psalm 23:3

It was an unbelievably beautiful morning in the spring. A golden sun was climbing in a brilliant blue, cloudless sky, and the sunlight sparkled in the cool air. Bob and I had decided to have our breakfast out on the patio, where our little fountain was dancing amid containers of pansies and mums.

Smiling at each other, we drank our orange juice and enjoyed the quiet beginning of a perfect day. Little curls of steam rose from our freshly buttered muffins as Bob read a page from a devotional for husbands and wives. We each enjoyed a cantaloupe half as we chatted about the grandchildren and the garden. Then, as we lingered over our fragrant cups of coffee, Bob pulled out our jar of Mom's Canned Questions.

A friend of ours developed this wonderful little product, which we sell at our More Hours in My Day seminars. It's really just a decorated jar full of little slips of paper, but each slip contains a question designed to stimulate thought and discussion. We use it often when we have company and when we are by ourselves, and the questions have brought us both tears and laughter as they helped us know each other better.

As usual, Bob drew out a question and passed the jar to me. I reached in and pulled out a slip. And then I seemed to feel dark clouds rolling in to block the sunshine as I read my question. My impulse was to say "Forget it" and stuff that little slip of paper back in the jar.

What was on the paper?

Just this: "What would you do if you could spend one day with your dad?"

Such a simple question. But the memories it evoked had the power to fill my cup with pain and anger and resentment.

You see, my dad was a brilliant man, a creative Viennese chef. He used to get standing ovations for the food he prepared. From what I'm told, he doted on me as a little child, and I've inherited some of his creativity in the kitchen.

And yet my dad was also a raging alcoholic. Living in our home meant always living on edge, never knowing when he might explode. One wrong word from any of us, and the spaghetti sauce would be dumped down the toilet or down the sink; the pots and pans would be whipped off the stove and the plates off the table. There would be shouting; there would be arguments. And although my father never physically abused me, he did take his rage out on my mother and brother.

In response to my father's rage, I almost gave up talking. If saying the wrong thing could trigger an explosion, I reasoned perhaps it was better not to say anything at all. So I became intensely introverted and fearful, and I wished my father dead many times. When I was eleven, he really did die, leaving a cloud of guilt and resentment that hung over my life long after I thought I had forgotten.

Even after my dad died, I still didn't talk much. When I met Bob and we began dating, he used to say to me, "Emilie, you've got to talk." And then so many wonderful things began to happen in my life. The most important was that Bob introduced me to Jesus, and I became a Christian. Then Bob asked me to marry him, and my Jewish mama (who was very wise) surprised me by giving her consent. Relatives criticized her for letting her precious sixteen-year-old marry a Gentile, but my mama sensed that Bob could give me the love and stability I needed.

Mama was right. After Bob and I were married and I felt secure for the first time in my life, I began to talk. Now I even talk for a living—and there are probably times when Bob wishes I would stop talking!

Our lives went on. Little Brad was born, then Jenny, and I threw my energy into raising our children and making a home for us all. Bob worked as an educator, then a businessman. The kids grew up and left home. Through an amazing series of events, More Hours in My Day became a book, then an exciting ministry. My mother came to know the Messiah and moved in with us. Grandbabies were born.

Through it all, I didn't think all that much about my dad. He was in my past, which I had put behind me. I was a Christian, and I knew I was supposed to forgive others. I read in the Bible that we had to forgive if God were going to forgive us. So yes, I forgave my dad—or so I thought.

And then one day Florence Littauer invited me to go to a seminar that her friend Lana Bateman was conducting at a nearby hotel. I didn't really know what it was about, only that Florence thought it would be good for anyone. So I just walked into that hotel room . . . and almost immediately the tears began to flow.

The spirit of God had prepared my heart for a remarkable experience in coming to terms with my past and growing closer to him. Part of what I realized that weekend was that I still had a lot of pain concerning my father. I thought I had forgiven him when I had really only boxed up my anger and resentment and stored it away—like sealing a bunch of toxic waste in a barrel and burying it underground. In order truly to forgive, I had to bring out that anger and resentment and actually hand them over to God, trusting him to take them away from me.

That weekend I began the process of truly forgiving my father and letting God restore my relationship with him. I admitted to myself that I needed healing. Even though my dad was long dead, I wrote him a long letter, pouring out both my love and my fury. I confessed the anger and bitterness I had held onto for so long without even knowing it was there.

All this was hard work. It demanded all my courage, all my energy. But what a difference that weekend made in my life. I poured out my cup of resentment. I let the Lord wash it bright and clean, and then I knew the awestruck wonder of having my cup filled to the brim with sparkling forgiveness—forgiveness for my father, and forgiveness for myself. What a wonderful feeling! I was clean, washed clean, drinking from a clean cup.

But that was not the end of the story.

Not long afterward, someone mentioned my father. And I was shocked to recognize the quick flash of anger, the stubborn, involuntary clenching of my jaw. The resentment was still there, or it had come back.

What was going on? Was that whole difficult weekend in vain?

Hadn't I emptied my cup of bitterness and let God fill it with forgiveness?

Oh yes!

The forgiveness I experienced that weekend was real. But now I was learning something very important about my cup of forgiveness.

It leaks!

For most of us, most of the time, forgiveness is an ongoing process, not a "done deal." Forgiveness is an absolute necessity for healthy living, the only known antidote to the bitterness and resentment and anger that flow naturally and abundantly when selfish human beings rub up against other selfish human beings.

But my cup of forgiveness seems to be one of the leakiest cups I own. It can be brimming over one day and empty the next—or refilled with bitter resentment over the very same hurt I thought I had forgiven. In fact, I can quickly accumulate enough pain and hurt and resentment to fill several cups, stacked up and precariously balanced.

All this can be discouraging.

"God, I thought I had let go of that!"

"God, I really want to forgive. Why is it so hard?"

But it can also be a source of faith, a reminder that we must keep going back to our forgiving Father for this cleansing elixir. We can't manufacture it ourselves; it always comes by the grace of God.

I love King David's beautiful song of forgiveness, Psalm 51. David's life was filled with one sin after another—things that were done to him and things that he did to others. But he knew the secret of coming to God for forgiveness. "Create in me a clean heart, O God," he prayed. He asked God not only to forgive, but to "wash me . . . whiter than snow."

How beautiful our cup can be when we offer it to the Lord—washed and cleaned, white and pure as the fresh-fallen snow, filled to the brim with beautiful, sparkling forgiveness. Why would we ever want to hold on to our scummy resentment when we could drink from that shining cup?

A friend of mine recently shared with me a great picture of how God's forgiveness works.

This friend works as a parent-aide in her daughter's third-grade class, and on one particular day she was assisting in an art lesson—a watercolor class. Each eight-year-old was given a piece of paper, a box of watercolors, a brush, a bowl of water, and a little plate for mixing colors. They were urged to experiment with colors and brush strokes, using the bowls of water to moisten the colors and to clean their brushes.

But it didn't take more than one or two dips of the brush for the water in the bowls to turn a murky gray—what the teacher called a "shadow color." And once the water was dirty, it contaminated the brighter colors. The yellows were especially vulnerable; one touch of the dark water, and the sunny yellow watercolor cake turned an ugly blackish-green.

What they needed, of course, was fresh water. So the teacher and the parent helpers began a process of moving around the room, systematically emptying the bowls and refilling the bowls with fresh water. It was a never-ending task, since the first bowls were dirty again long before the last bowls were refilled. And a few of the children didn't want their bowls refilled; they *liked* turning their paintings into muddy quagmires of brown and black. But most of the children were thrilled with the clean water, and they painted with zest, producing colorful original creations.

I've learned that forgiveness works that way, too.

I hold up my cup to be filled with sparkling clean forgiveness. And almost immediately, the resentment is creeping in—shadowy grudges from past dark memories or anger at new slights. The process of emptying out the resentment and being filled with forgiveness is an ongoing one. It has to happen again and again—as Jesus told his disciples, "seventy times seven."

Sometimes I don't want to let go of my resentment; I grow fond of my dark, murky attitudes. But when I allow an infilling of fresh "water," I am set free to live a full, creative life.

Interestingly enough, forgiveness works this way in our lives whether we're the forgivers or the "forgivees." Actually, the distinction is not all that clear, because every one of us has need to be both. Like the colors in a watercolor painting, forgiving and being forgiven run together, creating surprising and unforgettable patterns.

Every single one of us, because we are human and sinful and make mistakes and act out of motives that are less than pure, has a continual need to ask forgiveness of God and other humans.

Every single one of us, because the people around us are human and sinful and make mistakes and act out of motives that are less than pure, has constant need to forgive—or to ask God for the ability to forgive.

(We need to ask because all forgiveness—whether offered or received—is a gift of God. I can no more muster honest forgiveness on my own than my favorite teacup can fill itself with apple-cinnamon tea.)

Forgiveness, then, is an ongoing process of filling our leaky little cups. But that isn't the whole story. Forgiveness is ongoing, but it's not an endless, repetitive cycle. Instead, forgiveness has a forward motion. It's more like a couple gracefully waltzing across the room than a dog chasing its tail.

Things change as we practice the process of forgiveness. Over time, specific hurts lose their power to hurt us (and some hurts really are healed at the moment of forgiveness). More important, emptying out anger becomes a habit. We become less likely to let hurts fester, and we become more careful of the feelings of others. More and more we grow to understand what it's like to lead a clean life. Forgiving, and being forgiven, we waltz forward along in the paths of righteousness.

My friend who helped with the art class did not have to go around emptying water bowls forever. By the time she had made several rounds, the children were learning to wipe their brushes before dipping them in the water. Beautiful pictures were emerging on the papers—a purple whale swimming in a sunset sea, a fat orange pumpkin smiling on an emerald lawn, a swirling pattern of purple and blue designs. As more paintings neared completion, there were fewer bowls to be emptied. Some of the kids who were finished even started helping with the cleanup. The class was moving along.

We never, in this life, reach a point where we don't need to forgive.

We never reach a point where we don't need forgiveness.

But we do, if we are depending on God, move closer to completion, closer to that beautiful picture he wants to paint in the world through us. We move closer to him, and we learn to follow him better.

Forgiveness is a ongoing process, but it's not an endless cycle.

I need to remember that today, because I am struggling to forgive someone I love very much. She has done some things I don't approve of, and she has hurt others whom I also love. I know that I need to forgive her, and I also need forgiveness for ways I have acted toward her. And I know this forgiveness won't come in an easy, once-and-for-all act. The hurt is too deep, the pain too immediate.

But I know forgiveness can happen, and I know the pain can heal, and I know that I can move closer and closer to forgiveness.

I know, because of what happened with my attitude toward my dad.

You see, despite the dark cloud in my soul that darkened the breakfast sunshine that morning with Bob, I really was learning to fill my cup with forgiveness. And when I read that difficult question from the jar, I felt some pain, but I did have an answer.

What would I do if I could spend a day with my dad?

First of all, I would take his hand, and we would walk and talk. "Remember, daddy?" I would say, and we would reminisce about when I was a little girl. "Remember the times you would set me up on the counter next to you while you worked? Remember when you'd take me through those big doors into the kitchens full of those great, shining pots and pans?" I always felt so proud when my daddy would introduce me to the chefs as his little girl. I always felt so safe when he held my hand.

"And, oh, daddy, I'm so sorry!" I'd tell my dad if I could spend a day with him. "I'm sorry for all the terrible things that happened to you, all the things that hurt you and made you the way you were." And I'd say, "Daddy, I know why you drank. I know why you were full of fury. You had so much pain in your heart, in your cup—from being abandoned when your parents died and being raised in the kitchen in the palace of Vienna. And you have so much pain from being a Jew in Nazi-occupied Austria, and having to change your name to escape, and fighting in the war and being shot three times."

Daddy used to show us the scars from those gunshot wounds, but it was the deeper, hidden scars that caused him more pain. In so many ways his life was nothing but a battle. No wonder he tried to blot it out with alcohol.

If I could spend a day with my dad, I wouldn't want to deny the pain that he caused me. It was real, and I've learned that denying real pain hinders forgiveness instead of helping it. But I would also want to tell my dad that I love him. I would want to thank him for what he gave me—my creativity, my talent with food, the love he poured on me when he wasn't drinking.

And more than anything else, I would want to tell my dad that we have a heavenly Father who can cover the hurt and pain and take it from us. I would want him to know, more than anything else, my dearest friend, the Messiah, the Lord Jesus, the One who said, "Forgive, and you will be forgiven" (Luke 6:37).

I can't do that, of course. I can't spend another day with my dad, and that will always be a source of sadness for me. But I know I have finally come to a place in my life where memories of him are no longer a source of bitterness for me. Forgiveness has finally cleansed the area of my heart where those memories reside. And because that is true, I am more confident that other areas can be cleansed as well. Because I know forgiveness works, I am more ready to waltz another round.

Forgiveness works, even when you can't tell it's working. Even when you don't feel forgiven or don't feel forgiving. Even when you don't particularly want to forgive, when you find yourself grumping to God, "All right, I'll forgive since you say so, but . . ."

And forgiveness works no matter what the forgiveness issues are in your life.

Perhaps your spouse has been unfaithful or your son has adopted a lifestyle you cannot approve. Perhaps a friend has said something cruel behind your back or a colleague has attacked you publicly. Perhaps you are struggling with ongoing bitterness over something that happened years ago.

Or perhaps you need forgiveness for yourself. Perhaps you are overwhelmed with guilt or simply miserable because a relationship has been ruptured. Perhaps you are furious with yourself over a thoughtless remark, or you are beginning to be convicted of a hidden sin that is keeping you from fellowship with God.

Whatever in your life is causing you pain, you don't need to let resentment fill your cup. Above all, you don't need to hold on to the bitter brew.

Forgiveness works. You can take your cup to the Lord and ask him to empty it of resentment and guilt, to fill it with sparkling forgiveness. In Christ you can find the strength, if it's appropriate, to go to the other people involved and ask for forgiveness—and you can find the grace to accept forgiveness from God if the other person is not ready to grant it. Even if the other people involved are no longer in your life—or no longer living—you can write them a letter and pour out your heart. Do whatever it takes to remove the cloud and cleanse your soul and set you again on the paths of rightness.

Be prepared to do it again, if necessary—even seventy times seven times. But remember that if you've asked, God has answered. First John 1:9 assures us, "If we confess our sins, He is faithful and just to forgive us our sins and to cleanse us from all unrighteousness."

This is so vital to remember in those times when, for one reason or another, the forgiveness doesn't seem to be working.

I know of a woman who went through a bad time in her marriage and made a series of painful mistakes. She fell apart emotionally, the marriage split up, and her husband was granted custody of their two young children. Although she wrote them faithfully, they were very angry and wanted nothing to do with her.

Unfortunately, her ex-husband was very bitter and inflamed these feelings of anger. Eventually he moved them to a state so distant that she could barely afford to visit (although she tried).

During all this time, the woman worked very hard to rebuild her life. She relied on a competent counselor and support groups. She also returned to the faith she had left behind many years earlier. On her knees she expressed her repentance to God and begged forgiveness for her part in all that had happened. She also wrote her children and asked their forgiveness for anything she had done to hurt them.

After that, the problems continued. Her ex-husband was still hostile, and he even used her requests for forgiveness to try to deny her visitation. Her children were still distant. They were so far away that visits were a severe financial hardship. She struggled with guilt for what she had done and deep worry about her children's future.

So she went to her pastor with her pain.

"I've asked God to forgive me," she said. "And I really think he has. So why don't I feel forgiven? And why is everything still so hard?"

That wise pastor looked at her with great compassion. "If you've asked the Lord for forgiveness, he *has* forgiven you. So maybe what you need now is not forgiveness, but the grace to live with the consequences of your actions."

That has been a very helpful word for me during the times in my life when forgiveness just doesn't seem to work.

Forgiveness is not a superglue for broken relationships. It's not an eraser for hurtful remarks or painful memories. And forgiveness doesn't excuse us from having to cope with the consequences of sin in our lives and the lives of others.

Forgiveness works, but it works at the soul level, sometimes deeper than we can see. And that is why forgiveness doesn't seem to change anything—at least not right away.

True forgiveness—given or received—works because it changes me.

But that, of course, changes everything.

Savoring God's Word . . .
A Taste of Forgiveness

The kingdom of heaven is like a certain king who wanted to settle accounts with his servants. And when he had begun to settle accounts, one was brought to him who owed him ten thousand talents. But as he was not able to pay, his master commanded that he be sold, with his wife and children and all that he had, and that payment be made. The servant therefore fell down before him, saying, "Master, have patience with me, and I will pay you all." Then the master of that servant was moved with compassion, released him, and forgave him the debt. But that servant went out and found one of his fellow servants who owed him a hundred denarii; and he laid hands on him . . . , saying, "Pay me what you owe!" So his fellow servant fell down at his feet and begged him, saying, "Have patience with me, and I will pay you all." And he would not, but went and threw him into prison till he should pay the debt. So when his fellow servants saw what had been done, they were very grieved, and came and told their master all that had been done. Then his master, after he had called him, said to him, "You wicked servant! I forgave you all that debt because you begged me. Should you not also have had compassion on your fellow servant, just as I had pity on you?"

Matthew 18:23–33

Have mercy upon me, O God,
According to Your lovingkindness;
According to the multitude of Your tender mercies,
Blot out my transgressions.
Wash me thoroughly from my iniquity,
And cleanse me from my sin. . . .
Behold, You desire truth in the inward parts,
And in the hidden part You will make me to know wisdom.
Purge me with hyssop, and I shall be clean;
Wash me, and I shall be whiter than snow. . . .
Hide Your face from my sins,
And blot out all my iniquities.
Create in me a clean heart, O God,
And renew a steadfast spirit within me.
Do not cast me away from Your presence,
And do not take Your Holy Spirit from me.
Restore to me the joy of Your salvation,
And uphold me with Your generous Spirit.
Then I will teach transgressors Your ways,
And sinners shall be converted to You.

Psalm 51: 1-13

Fill my cup, Lord . . .

I offer you my cup of fear

and worry and overcontrol

that you may fill it with trust.

4

A Cup of Trust

Yea, though I walk through the valley
of the shadow of death,
I will fear no evil . . .
Psalm 23:3

One day Bob and I were in our van, trying to cross a really busy highway. There was no traffic light at this particular intersection, and the cars were whizzing by right and left. Bob was craning his neck, trying to find an opening. I didn't want to add to his worries, so I just sat quietly.

We sat there for several minutes with Bob poised to make his move. Finally he saw his opening and zipped out across the road. We made it!

As we continued on our way, Bob looked over at me. "You know, Em, I noticed you weren't even looking at all those cars. Weren't you worried we wouldn't get across?"

"Oh," I said without thinking, "I trust you."

Bob's questioning expression turned into a beaming smile. "Thank you," he said.

I was a little surprised by his enthusiastic response. But when I thought about it a little more, I understood why he was so pleased.

You see, trust is a compliment. It's a gesture of respect, a gift of esteem. And it's a gift not lightly given, because trust is also a risk. Trusting someone means giving that person a little bit of control over our lives—which means that other person may let us down.

That's why the trust of a child is so poignant. When a little one reaches up and takes my hand, I feel a little tug at my heartstrings because I know she's giving me the gift of her trust. She's trusting that I will help her and not hurt her, that I will meet her needs. Then I feel a surge of responsibility, because I know just how vulnerable that little child is. And I also feel a little stab of pain because I know this world can be so untrustworthy.

"Hey, trust me." Can you even hear the words without feeling a tingle of distrust? These days it seems we're bombarded with all the bad things that can happen if we let down our guard and trust *anybody*. We can be bilked or conned. We can be cheated, mugged, even murdered.

And we don't even need to leave home to be let down. Anyone who has ever lived in a relationship knows that. A promise broken, a responsibility shirked, a word spoken or not spoken—friends and families can betray each other with devastating accuracy. We do it out of carelessness, out of cruelty, out of our own mistrust.

I can still taste the bitter cup of betrayal and disappointment and fear I drank as a young girl growing up with an alcoholic father. I knew that my daddy loved me, but I couldn't trust him to control himself, to be consistent with me. I couldn't even trust him to go on living. Daddy died when I was eleven—and to a child, the death of a parent feels like abandonment, the ultimate betrayal.

I also knew the agony of trust when one of my uncles violated my body. "Come sit with me," he would say, and when I obeyed he would begin fondling me. Eventually I would get up and leave the room. I don't know why I didn't kick or scream or tell my aunt—perhaps because I had been raised to obey all adults. But I still remember that deep sense of betrayal when someone I trusted hurt me.

But you don't need my stories to convince you it's an untrustworthy world. You have your own stories. You know what it is like to be betrayed by those to whom you gave the gift of your trust. And you know you have to "be careful out there."

And yet, not trusting is not an option—if we want to have any relationships at all. We can't be close to anyone without giving that person the gift of our trust. We have to take the risk, even when we know we could be hurt.

The crucial questions, of course, are who and how. Whom can I trust? And how can I manage to trust again when my trust has been betrayed?

When it comes to people, there aren't any guarantees. We can be wise when it comes to choosing the people we relate to, trusting in our own instincts and the counsel of others and the nudging of the Holy Spirit. We can follow some commonsense precautions—like letting relationships develop slowly and not giving credit card numbers to people who call—to keep from becoming involved with extremely untrustworthy people. But even those precautions can't keep us truly safe.

The trouble is that *everyone* is untrustworthy at one time or another. We *all* let each other down. So I think we need to look a little deeper when it comes to choosing whom and how we are going to trust.

When it comes to people, I think we need to look at character and intentions—and what we are trusting others to be and do.

You see, I do trust my husband, Bob. I trust him profoundly. And yet I don't trust him never to make a mistake. I don't trust him never to hurt my feelings or forget an appointment or utter an unkind word. I don't trust my Bob not to be human. If I did, I would be setting myself up for long-term disappointment and bitterness.

What I do trust is Bob's fundamental character. I trust him to be the kind and competent man I know him to be. I trust him to want to stay in relationship with me, to want the best for me. I trust him to learn from his mistakes and to continue to grow.

And how do I know what Bob's character is like and what his intentions are? He's shown me! Over and over again in our life together he has shown that he can be trusted. Even before I met him or knew him well, I knew him by reputation. Mutual friends assured me that he was "all right." I also believe the Holy Spirit was working in my heart, softening it and allowing me to trust in the man God had chosen for me.

All of this brings me to the issue of trusting God. And sometimes I think it's a lot harder for me to trust God than it is to trust an imperfect (but wonderful) human like Bob. After all, God is a spirit. I can't touch him or smell him or see him. Like most people, I have my moments when I doubt he even exists.

And yet I need to trust God if I am going to live in relationship with him. I need to trust God in order to trust anyone else—for how else can I have the security to give the gift of my trust to people I know might let me down?

So how can I trust God?

Basically, it works with God the way it works with Bob.

I trust God because of what he is like, because of what he has done. And I know these things both from my own experience and from what I have seen in the lives of others. I can trust God because he has shown me who he is and what his intentions are toward me and all his people. Over and over, by his Word and his actions, he has shown that he is a God who can be trusted.

The holy Scriptures give dramatic witness to God's trustworthiness. The psalmist and the prophets and the gospels say it in pictures. The Lord is my rock. He is my help and shield. He is my redeemer. He is the bread of life, the living water, the good shepherd, the way and the truth and the life.

The Scriptures say it in story, too. Once upon a time there was a God who created human beings and chose a specific group of people to belong to him and show him to the world. Over the centuries this God cared for his people and rescued them and disciplined them and persistently loved them even when they turned their backs on him. And then this God made the ultimate commitment, passed the ultimate test of character and intent. He sent his only son to die for those people—to show us just how deeply he can be trusted.

To me the most incredible part in this whole incredible scriptural story is that I'm part of it. I, too, am created and rescued and disciplined and loved and redeemed by God. I, too, have a part in God's story. And my part, is in essence, to trust him, to let him work in my life and change me and guide me.

This really is a God I can trust. He's shown me by what he has done in the lives of so many people I know. Again and again, in the face of pain and doubt and despair, my God has proved himself trustworthy—I've seen it happen.

I think of my friend Carol Thornburg, who lost her beloved husband five years ago. They were so close, and she was so dependent on him, and I wondered how she would ever learn to function alone. But what a privilege it has been to see the ways God has provided for my friend through the years. He has taken her step-by-step from selling a house to buying a house to selling a house to being financially comfortable enough to volunteer her time in Christian ministry. In the five years she has been on her own, so she has learned to trust the Lord for her needs. And she has figured it out so that she has just enough money to live on while she gives away her time in the Lord's work.

And I think of others as well. Marilyn Heavilyn, who lost three sons and almost lost a grandbaby yet has touched so many through her testimony to God's goodness. Or Joni Eareckson Tada, who became a quadriplegic as a teenager but who speaks and writes and draws and sings so eloquently about God's goodness. Or Janis Willis, whose six children were killed in a highway accident but who managed to say, "I realized I had been saying, 'no, no, no,' to God as my children were entering heaven's doors. I was saying 'no God' to the very thing I ultimately wanted most for our children—to be with God eternally. . . . We have thrown ourselves into God's grace."[1]

And of course my own experience reminds me again and again that God can be trusted. Again and again in my life he has given me exactly what I needed in order to grow and move toward him.

This is a God who took a little girl with good reason to distrust men and healed that distrust by giving her a husband who is strong and dependable and nurturing.

This is a God who took a willing but inexperienced young wife and put her in charge of a household of five small children—an effective crash course in home organization—then gave her the opportunity and the encouragement to teach others what she had learned.

This is a God who took a restless empty-nest mom and gave her a nationwide ministry of writing and speaking.

And this is a God who, again and again, has given me the gift of his presence when I gave him the gift of my trust. When I look back at the way my life has unfolded, I can only be astonished at the wisdom and creativity of my heavenly Father.

This really is a God I can trust. In my life he has shown me again and again that he is a rock and a help and a shield, the way and the truth and the life.

And that raises another question.

Why do I still have such a hard time trusting God?

Why do I keep falling back into paralyzing fears and agonizing worries—as if God can't take care of me? Why do I keep trying to control my circumstances and my loved ones—as if God can't take care of them as well as me? Why do I keep acting as if this great trustworthy God were not capable of running the universe?

This last kind of distrust has always been a trap for me. Maybe it comes from having so much responsibility in my young life or from learning to be distrustful. But I tend to want everything to be right and good and perfect, and if things aren't running the way I think they should I tend to move in and take over. Do I want to control other people's lives when they're not moving in the direction I think they should.

No, I don't think that consciously. I just act that way. I've done it again and again in my life—given God my trust and then taken it back and tried to run things myself.

But I am learning. I am moving forward in my ability to trust. And God is helping me do it.

You see, what I am learning is that although my trust is a gift I offer to God, I cannot offer it unless he gives it to me first. He is the source from whom all blessings flow; I cannot offer him anything he didn't originate. And yet my offering is very important.

It's like a small child buying a gift for her mother. Where does the money come from the first place? Even if she draws her mother a picture, the crayons and the paper and even the little girl's talent came from the mother. And yet the act of giving brings such joy to both mother and child—and the child is learning valuable lessons at the same time.

So I give what I can. I offer to this great, trustworthy God my cup of fear and worry and overcontrol. As I hold it up to him, my cup is emptied and filled with trust and handed back to me—so I can offer it back to him. And then I must offer my cup of trust back to him.

But I don't want to get too caught up in pretty pictures here. How specifically do I hold up my cup to be filled with trust?

One way is through prayer. I need to be offering up my cup daily in the form of prayer for my family, for my church, for my children. I need to pray that they will fear the Lord and serve him. And then—this is the hardest part—I need to relinquish them, to give over those concerns to the Lord as a gesture of trust. I need to learn to pray, "God, I pray that you will do whatever it takes to transform our son or daughter or grandchild into a person who will serve you, know you, and love you with all his heart, mind, and soul. I don't know what we will have to experience before that happens. But that is my prayer."

So prayer is an offering of trust, a way to hold up my cup for filling with more trust. So is patience, being willing to wait, even when the urge to take over is strong.

I have always found it especially hard to trust God when I think something should be happening—and it isn't. Those times really tend to throw me. But I'm gradually learning to trust God even in those maddening waiting times. I've been able to look back and see that during some of those times when God didn't seem to be moving, I was moving in growth. Or I can see that if God had acted when I wanted him to, things would not have turned out so well; God's timing was far better than mine.

This brings me back again to trusting that God knows best, that he is capable of running the universe. When I wait patiently for the Lord to act in his own time, I am giving him the gift of my trust—and growing in my ability to trust.

Most of the time, though, it's not just a matter of waiting. Obedience—the willingness to follow God's nudges even when we don't completely understand why—is crucial. It's no accident that the old hymn was titled "Trust and Obey." They go together. And they're both hard. In fact, without God, they're impossible. Our cups are empty of all good things unless God is filling them.

But God does fill our cups when we hold them up. I'm learning that more and more these days. The recent unhappiness in my family has made me realize how weak my trust can be and how desperately I want to trust God. I am really seeking to trust him in every area of my life, from what happens in the next five minutes to what happens in the next five years.

And you know, the more I trust him, the more I'm learning to trust. The more I'm coming to know his character, to stare in amazement at what he's done in my life and wait in anticipation for what he's going to do next. I'm learning the truth that C. W. Christian expressed so eloquently:

> My faith is small.
> I measure it in dust
> And test its weight with straw
> And wonder that he pays me heed at all.
> How well I must
> In my self-serving supplication gall
> His patience with my feeble trust.
> Yet I in all fair expectation wait.
> My faith is small;
> My God is great.[2]

So I am learning a lot more about trust these days, and as a result, my life is much more peaceful. I also find that my perspective has sharpened; I have a clearer sense of the basic realities. I know who I can trust—and how.

I can trust God to care for me and help me grow. I can trust God to give me his presence in this life and then, when my life is over, to take me home to glory.

Most important, I can trust God to run the universe. (I don't have to.) That trust enables me to take a more lighthearted attitude toward all that concerns me.

Take my teacups, for instance.

The collection of teacups in my armoire and all around the house is one of my signatures—one of the things I'm known for. I've spoken about my teacups, and written about them. They are full of memories and very precious to me, and I've always been very protective of them. But a few years ago I realized that my time was more valuable. To write or speak or minister, I needed to relinquish my house to someone who could clean for me. Relinquishing the task of cleaning the armoire with the teacups was the hardest. How could I trust anyone else with my precious collection?

Well, not long after I gave up the task, my fears were realized. The housekeeper put the shelf back in wrong; it slipped and broke some of the teacups. That was a traumatic day. But when I took my pain to God, trusting him with it, he gently and gradually changed my attitude.

I still love my teacups, but I'm not nearly as vigilant about them anymore. Now I reassure my housekeeper, "Don't be afraid of the teacups." (And I know she is more careful with them than I am.) Now I'm more likely to let little children drink tea out of my cups, to give them the gift of my trust along with the assurance that an accident won't cause me to love them any less.

For many years I have had tea parties with my granddaughter, Christine. Her brothers Chad and Bevan have enjoyed their tea parties, too. And recently when our little two-and-a-half-year-old Bradley Joe was over at the house I had a tea party with him, trusting him to drink very carefully out of one of my china teacups. I knew he could easily break that delicate cup. But I wanted to take that risk to show him how special he was to me. And he got the message. He went home and told his mother excitedly about his grownup tea party with Grammy. Even in his baby mind, he sensed he was being trusted and he tried his best to live up to it.

And that gives me a little insight, too, into how my relationship with God works—how he fills my cup with trust.

This most trustworthy God teaches me to trust—by trusting me!

Remember, real trust is a gift you give to someone you love. It's a compliment, a gesture of respect. And it's also a way of helping them grow, to become more trustworthy.

Or put another way, when I choose to live in relationship with someone, I have to give the gift of my trust—or it's not really a relationship, just a contract.

If an employee embezzles or doesn't show up for work, it hurts the employer in the pocketbook. If that employee is also a friend, if you have a relationship, the embezzlement or absence is a betrayal of trust.

You don't have trust unless you have a relationship.

And because he wants a relationship with me, the trustworthy God who created the universe has trusted me to do his work in the world!

He has entrusted me with a family and friends and charged me with living in a way that helps them draw close to them. He has entrusted me with the job of ministry—with the women I speak to and the people who read my books and also the people I meet in the course of my everyday life. He has entrusted me with his love so that I can have a relationship with him and with others.

Do I abuse that trust?

Of course. I do it every day.

I abuse God's trust whenever I ignore one of those little nudgings of the Holy Spirit to go see someone or help someone. I abuse his trust when I snap at Bob or criticize one of my children. I abuse his trust when I fail to trust him.

But that's sort of beside the point because, in this world, if trust depended on trust never being betrayed—we'd never trust anybody. If I waited until I was sure the grandchildren would never break a teacup, I would never have a tea party with them.

Trusting is a risk you take in the interest of love. It's a calculated gamble, risking betrayal in the interest of the other person's growth. You don't necessarily trust that the other person won't do wrong, but you do trust that the person will stay in relationship with you and grow. You trust that person's basic character and potential. You trust who the person is, and who the person can be.

And that's what God does with us. The very fact that we have a life is an astounding vote of confidence on God's part. The fact that we have free will is an amazing act of trust. He's trusting that we will come to him! He's giving us room to grow.

When I was a little girl, I would sometimes wake up in the middle of the night and need to go to the bathroom. It was dark. We didn't have a night-light. So I would call out in the darkness.

"Mama, I need to go."

"Well, then, go," she would answer, her voice close and warm.

"But it's dark. I'm afraid."

Her reply came gently, assuring me of her presence, trusting me to grow.

"Be afraid," she would say, "but go."

More and more, as I grow older, I've become aware of God's love and trust working like that in my life. He allows the pain and the fear and the struggle because he trusts me to grow through them. But he's always present, a comforting, trustworthy voice in the darkness, telling me:

"Be afraid, but go. There is no place you can go that I won't be.

"Go ahead," he says. "You can trust me."

And I can.

Savoring God's Word . . .
A Taste of Trust

You will keep him in perfect peace, whose mind is stayed on You, because he trusts in You.

Isaiah 26:3

I will both lie down in peace, and sleep; for You alone, O Lord, make me dwell in safety.

Psalm 4:8

The Lord is my strength and my shield;
My heart trusted in Him, and I am helped;
Therefore my heart greatly rejoices,
And with my song I will praise Him.

Psalm 28:7

Not that we are sufficient of ourselves to think of anything as being from ourselves, but our sufficiency is from God.

2 Corinthians 3:5

"Ah, Lord God! Behold, You have made the heavens and the earth by Your great power and outstretched arm. There is nothing too hard for You.

Jeremiah 32:17

Consider the lilies of the field, how they grow; they neither toil nor spin; and yet I say to you that even Solomon in all his glory was not arrayed like one of these. Now if God so clothes the grass of the field, which today is, and tomorrow is thrown into the oven, will He not much more clothe you, O you of little faith? Therefore do not worry, saying, 'What shall we eat?' or 'What shall we drink?' or 'What shall we wear?' For after all these things the Gentiles seek. For your heavenly Father knows that you need all these things. But seek first the kingdom of God and His righteousness, and all these things shall be added to you."

Matthew 6:28-33

Do not fret because of evildoers,
Nor be envious of the workers of iniquity. . . .
Trust in the Lord, and do good;
Dwell in the land, and feed on His faithfulness.
Delight yourself also in the Lord,
And He shall give you the desires of your heart.
Commit your way to the Lord,
Trust also in Him,
And He shall bring it to pass.
He shall bring forth your righteousness as the light,
And your justice as the noonday.
Rest in the Lord, and wait patiently for Him. . . .
For evildoers shall be cut off;
But those who wait on the Lord,
They shall inherit the earth.

Psalm 37

Fill my cup, Lord . . .

I offer you my cup of loneliness and

selfishness, that you may

give me your cup of communion.

5

A Cup of Communion

You are with me.

Psalm 23:4

It's one of my favorite times of day.

The sun has set. The phone has stopped ringing. (I hope!) The conference schedules are filed away, and the dishwasher is finishing up the last of the mealtime chores. A little fire in the fireplace chases away the chill, while a string quartet plays merrily on the CD.

Bob is comfortable in his big green leather easy chair, an afghan on his lap and a book in his hand. Every few minutes he stops to read me a passage while I putter in the kitchen, preparing our evening cup of tea.

I don't hurry as I pour the boiling water into the teapot. The delightful scent of cinnamon starts to waft around the kitchen as I gather together lace napkins, china cups, sugar, and cream. A candle in a crystal holder casts a golden glow, a single daisy plucked from an arrangement in the hall smiles from a miniature vase. I rummage quietly in the pantry to find a few cookies, and I know there's a bunch of grapes in the refrigerator.

The tea is steeped. I carry the tray into our peaceful living room.

Bob moves his feet from the hassock to make room for the tray. I curl up on the carpet beside him and pour. And then while the fire crackles and the music dances, we talk quietly or we pray or we just sit and share our cup of cinnamon and sharing—our delicious cup of communion.

Communion, you see, is not just another name for the Lord's Supper—although the ritual of bread and wine embodies that reality on the most profound level.

Communion is also the appropriate word for what happens whenever spirits are shared and cups are filled with love and mutual participation. It's what happens whenever human beings draw near to each other and to God, managing somehow to emerge from their separateness and partake of the shared life God intended.

You see, God never intended for us to be alone. He said that from the beginning. He made us for each other and for fellowship with him.

Our separateness, our deep-seated loneliness, that familiar sense of being all alone in a body with "me, me, me"—that's our own doing. It's the long-term result of that long-ago choice to listen to a serpent, eat an apple, take charge of our own destiny. Because we are sinful, there's a part of us that always wants to hide from God and each other.

And then we feel so alone, even in the midst of a crowd. Even in the bustle of our work, the warmth of our families. By ourselves we are just ourselves, and our cups are full of ourselves only.

That's why those moments of true communion are so delicious. They are a pure gift, a generous outpouring from the God whose very nature is relationship. (For what is the holy Trinity but an intertwined relationship of three identities—Father, Son, and Holy Spirit?) It is my loving Lord who empties my cup of loneliness and selfishness and pours for me my cup of communion.

That doesn't mean that people who don't know God cannot enjoy moments of special sharing or even deep connection. It doesn't mean you have be a Christian in order to enjoy closeness and friendship. In a sense, the cup of communion is a gift from creation, part of how we are made. God created us to connect to each other, and even our sinful separation has not negated that built-in capacity. God made us with the need for other people and the desire to live in harmony instead of discord, sharing instead of separation, fulfillment instead of loneliness. He created us with the physical and emotional tools we need to connect with each other—eyes, hands, voices, sympathy, loyalty, understanding. Human beings do manage to make some connections with each other while living apart from God.

And yet there is something so different, something so special about the cup of communion that is poured for me when I bring my cup of loneliness to the throne of God and hold it up to be washed and refilled with sharing and closeness and love. It's like the difference between muddy pond water and water from a flowing spring. It sparkles.

That's why, although I may have good and even loving relationships with men and women who don't know Christ—and there are many in my family—the relationships I share with my Christian brothers and sisters are different. It's more than just having a belief or a cause in common. It's having a *life* in common. When even two or three of us are gathered in the Lord's name, the presence of the Holy Spirit adds a sparkling eternal dimension to our human communion.

I cannot even begin to imagine what our marriage would be like without that eternal dimension. My Bob, who is very wise, knew from the beginning that we would have little chance of going the distance without having a closeness in that area. Even though he was attracted to me and respected my Jewish heritage, he held back. Instead of courting me, he shared his faith with me. And only when we had come to share a commitment to Jesus Christ as the Messiah did he propose marriage.

Over and over in my life I have thanked the Lord for Bob's strength and wisdom, for we have needed the spiritual communion of our shared faith to get through the tough times in our life together. My husband has always been my best friend, and being able to pray together and read Scripture together and talk together about the Lord and work together in ministry has been a privilege and a joy. In my marriage, God has poured out his cup of communion with overflowing generosity.

And there are other ways God fills my cup with communion. I have always loved sharing my faith with our children and especially with the grandchildren. I love to see them growing in the Lord, even through their painful experiences. In many ways they minister to me, and I rejoice to see that they have a spiritual foundation I never had at their age.

My church family, too, offers me so many opportunities to come out of my loneliness and share a cup of communion. Bob and I have developed deep and meaningful friendships in this body. I love the sense of spiritual sharing I feel when we sing and study and serve together, and especially when we gather together at the Lord's table to remember his ultimate act of sharing.

Even closer to my heart than my church family is my special adopted family of prayer partners. These are my close-to-the-heart friends whose love has stood the test of time. These are the people I call when my heart is aching, the ones I trust above all others to pray with me. They are all so different—Yoli and Barbara and Donna. But they are truly the sisters of my heart. They are the ones I trust not only with my tears, but with my puffy red eyes and unsightly runny nose and scrunched-up crying face. They have truly been God's gift of communion to me.

But my cup of communion is not just filled among the people I know. My kinship with other brothers and sisters in Christ has brought Bob and me into "family reunions" across the nation. This is one of the most amazing surprises God has given me over my lifetime (and there have been so many surprises!). He has used our ministry of teaching and writing not only to do his work of touching lives and reclaiming spirits, but also to fill our cups with sparkling Christian communion.

We are on the road nearly every week, traveling to lead seminars in towns we've never visited before. We've reached the point where we can almost predict what will happen. Someone we have never seen will meet us at the airport. For three or four days we will pray together and eat together and work together and perhaps live together with people with whom we may have little in common but a shared desire to serve the Lord. And then, by the time the weekend is over, our cup of communion will be filled. We are all fast friends. Sometimes we will end up being in touch for years.

It doesn't just happen with seminars, either. By God's grace, I have been able to share deeply with people I will never meet, women I encounter only as a voice on the phone or a face at a conference or a folded-up sheet of notepaper in an envelope. Somehow God uses what I say or do to touch these women. Somehow they find the courage to come to me with their pain. And somehow, as we talk together or pray together, he fills both our cups with a special kind of communion.

But perhaps you are a bit fed up by now with my litany of communion. Perhaps you are going through a lonely time. Perhaps you are grieving the loss of someone you loved or having difficulty making friends.

Perhaps you feel isolated and alone in the midst of your family or your church, and my stories about a close marriage or a loving church family or sympathetic friends just leave you feeling hollow.

I understand if you feel that way.

You see, the very reason my cups of communion seem so amazing is that my cup was very full of loneliness for most of my life. I am an introverted person by nature, and the pain of living in an alcoholic home wrapped me further in a shell of separateness. I grew up feeling different and alone, and I would never have considered bringing other children home to my disordered household. Then, after my father died, I was too busy trying to keep house for my mother and manage my schoolwork to have time for friends—even if I could come out of myself enough to make one.

And even though God in his amazing mercy has granted me the gift of a good marriage and good friendships, I don't always feel like my cup of communion is filled. There are many times when I struggle with a private grief in the midst of a public crowd. Sometimes I can be in church or with Bob and feel like I'm a million miles away. And I still find that my best friends are those who reach out to me first, those who don't wait for me to reach out to them.

My cup of communion—like so many of my "earthen vessel" cups—is a leaky one, and when the sharing drains away I often find I'm the same shy little girl who hid behind her mother's skirts.

I know I'm not the only one who feels this way. All of our cups are leaky when it comes to communion. Even though we were created for sharing, we are also flawed by the sin, and sin is separation—from God and from other human beings. We are made for relationships, but we are also selfish, and we suffer from the selfishness of others. We yearn to be close to others, but we are also lonely to the core, still locked inside our own skulls, unable on our own to truly understand or reach out.

So even though we were created for communion, communion is still a miracle.

Without the miracle of communion, friendships go flat, church friends betray each other, marriages dissolve into separateness or fall apart altogether. Without the miracle of communion I am left with only me. But with the miracle of communion I am filled.

And here's the biggest miracle of all. I don't have to make friends or influence people in order to have my cup filled with communion. I don't even need to be with other people.

Sometimes my heavenly Father does fill my cup of communion through my relationships with Bob or my children or my church or my prayer partners or the people who come to my seminars.

But always—with or without other people—he fills my cup of communion with himself. My most satisfying cup of sharing comes in my relationship with him.

I love the way Tracey St. John put it in her letter to a national columnist. Lynn Minton, in her column on youth in *Parade* magazine, had asked readers, "Do you believe in God?" This is what Tracey wrote:

> I was 17 when I left high school, depressed and without direction. I found myself pregnant and married a man who essentially reaffirmed that I was not going to amount to much. I later divorced him and continued making monumentally lousy decisions.
>
> Then I met someone, now my best friend. He too is a parent. He began to tell me that I was worth something. He listened as I expressed my disgust with what I had done with my life. At times, I even personally attacked him. But his patience was unbelievable. Today, I am a student in a very competitive medical program and a much better parent. I owe all my success to my best friend, who has been there every step of the way.
>
> So what does this have to do with whether I believe in God? Who do you think my best friend is?[1]

My life has been different from Tracey's, but her experience with God has been my experience, too.

1. Quoted in "Lynn Minton Reports: Fresh Voices," *Parade* (15 October 1995): 23.

Over the years, I have learned that Jesus is the One I can always trust, the One I can always talk to, the One whose love truly changes my life.

I know that I can talk to the Lord and say, "Today I'm not feeling that I can trust. Today I'm not sure that I like my Bob too much. Today I'm really upset with the children." The one thing I really have experienced with the Lord is that I can tell him anything, that he's not going to tell anybody else, and that he's going to comfort me and forgive and love me.

That's what a real friend is, isn't it?

A friend can love you in spite of who you are.

A friend can comfort you wherever you are.

A friend can speak to you in honesty but then encourage you to move on to the next step.

A friend can fill your cup with sharing and closeness and love—with communion.

The old hymn really had it right: "What a Friend We Have in Jesus."

The older I get, the more I long for that friendship with my Lord to grow. I realize there isn't any thing else on this earth that can give me more joy or fulfillment or strength. I want to talk with him, to share my life with him, to hold my cup of communion up to be filled with him. I want my Lord to use me, to live in me, to fill others' cups through me.

No, I don't always get it right. I don't always feel close to Jesus—anymore than I always feel close to Bob or our children or our fellow creatures. As long as I live in this sin-touched body and in this sin-touched world, my cup will leak.

That is why I must constantly pray—

Lord, I'm lonely. Fill my cup.

Lord, I've been so caught up in myself I can't even think about Bob or Jenny or Yoli or anybody else. Fill my cup.

Lord, I've been trying to do it all by myself again. I've been trying to go it on my own. And I don't want to do it anymore.

Fill my cup, Lord, with communion.

Fill my cup, Lord, with you.

Savoring God's Word . . .
A Taste of Communion

And the Lord God said, "It is not good that man should be alone."

Genesis 2:18

God sets the solitary in families;
He brings out those who are bound into prosperity;
But the rebellious dwell in a dry land.

Psalm 68:6

I say to you that if two of you agree on earth concerning anything that they ask, it will be done for them by My Father in heaven. For where two or three are gathered together in My name, I am there in the midst of them.

Matthew 18:19,20

The cup of blessing which we bless, is it not the communion of the blood of Christ? The bread which we break, is it not the communion of the body of Christ? For we, being many, are one bread and one body; for we all partake of that one bread.

I Corinthians 10:16,17

Jesus spoke these words, lifted up His eyes to heaven, and said, ". . . Holy Father, keep through Your name those whom You have given Me, that they may be one as We are. . . . I do not pray for these alone, but also for those who will believe in Me through their word; that they all may be one, as You, Father, are in Me, and I in You; that they also may be one in Us, that the world may believe that You sent Me."

John 17:1,11,20-22

No longer do I call you servants, for a servant does not know what his master is doing; but I have called you friends, for all things that I heard from My Father I have made known to you.

John 15:15

If we walk in the light as He is in the light, we have fellowship with one another, and the blood of Jesus Christ His Son cleanses us from all sin.

I John 1:7

I thank my God upon every remembrance of you.

Philippians 1:3

Fill my cup, Lord . . .

I offer you my cracked and

crumbling cup

that you may remold me

and make me strong.

6

A Cup of Strength

. . . Your rod and Your staff,
they comfort me.
Psalm 23:4

It was three o'clock in the afternoon on a day in early December. The chairs for our holiday seminar were being set up in the assembly hall. Our boxes and baskets of prayer planners and feather dusters and rubber "spootulas" were stacked behind the long tables, ready to be displayed and sold. Someone was on the stage, fiddling with the sound system. Someone else was putting up signs.

And me? I was in the process of coming unglued. Dissolving into tears. Totally losing it.

Now, hysterics are not normal for me, especially not right before a seminar. But I was drained from weeks of traveling, doing workshop after workshop in a series of different cities and churches. I was run-down from meeting people, giving to people, hauling books, and making bookings, and I was fighting a low-grade sinus infection that refused to go away. But I had really been looking forward to this seminar because it was here in our very own town, in our very own church, arranged for by people I knew and loved. This one was going to be easy and fun.

Then the woman in charge of the registration process called with a problem. Apparently we had overbooked the hall. Twelve hundred women had sent in their registration forms, and we had seats for only a thousand. The fire marshal had said no to putting in more chairs, so we would have to turn two hundred women away.

That little piece of bad news did it. My composure collapsed like a blob of warm jelly. All I could think of was those two hundred women.

"We can't turn them away," I sobbed. "God moved their hearts to want to come here; he must have a blessing for them. We can't turn them away from getting a blessing. Maybe there's somebody who really needs to be here tonight. We can't turn anybody away. We just can't . . ."

Without a word our friend Ellen, who helps us in our office and at our seminars, stepped close and took me in her arms. She pressed my head against her shoulder and murmured the way you do to a baby who is out of control.

"There, there, it's going to be all right."

And you know what? It was all right.

Ellen was God's strength to me at that moment. I leaned on her until I calmed down and regained control. Meanwhile, someone stepped in and began making plans for handling the overflow. Seats were found for the extra two hundred people. We even were able to accommodate two women from Oregon who just happened to walk in—although they literally had to sit in the bathroom and watch the seminar on closed-circuit TV.

I completed that weekend with an unusual sense of fulfillment and blessing. Not only did I sense God's presence in a special way during the sessions, but I was also profoundly grateful to Ellen and the others for ministering to me in a moment when life was just too much. And I was reminded in a vivid way of a truth I often want to ignore:

I don't have to be strong all the time.

In fact, God doesn't *want* me to be strong—at least not the way the world usually defines it.

God wants me to learn to lean on him the way I leaned on Ellen, the way a weary shepherd leans on his staff. He wants me to be comforted by his mighty power and to depend on him, not my jerky little efforts, to get through my life. He wants to fill my cup with the strong brew of his magnificent presence.

This is not a new insight. You've probably heard it before. You've heard that the Lord's strength is made perfect in weakness. It is. But what does that mean in terms of how we act and speak in our everyday lives?

Does God want us to *try* to be weak just so he can be strong?

No, that's not it at all. The point is not trying to be weak. The point is that we *are* weak.

We are cracked teacups, crumbling little earthenware creations, made in the divine image and gifted by God, but still weak, subject to breakage. We live in bodies that can break down. We are lazy, inconstant, stained with sin and selfishness, vulnerable to hate and pride and jealousy.

And God?

He is God! He is the creator of the universe, the One who keeps the galaxies whirling. He is the One who dreamed up blue whales and plankton, quantum physics and nuclear energy—and us. He was the One who opened the sea and raised Lazarus from the dead and then conquered death once and for all.

The simple little children's song sums it up succinctly:

> Little ones to him belong,
> They are weak but he is strong.

So the real issue here is not trying to be weak or strong, but getting a clear view of who we are and who God is.

The Bible doesn't tell us, "Be strong." And it doesn't tell us, "Be weak."

It tells us, "Look at who you are, and look at who God is." And then do the logical thing—which is to lean on him, to depend on his strength.

But it's not always easy to do. We are too brainwashed by the messages of the world: Be tough, get physical, command respect, don't let anyone walk all over you.

We're driven by fear, too. If we're not strong, we think, others will walk all over us. If we're not tough, we won't survive. We need our shell. We need our cocky confidence.

But here's another amazing paradox.

When we try to be strong on our own, we only end up showing how weak we really are. We become stiff and brittle or out of control. Even if we end up on top, we will eventually be toppled.

But when we take an alternate path, God's path, and let him be the strong one, an amazing thing happens. We admit our weakness and lean on him. And then . . . we become stronger.

I become a strong woman of God when I offer him my cup of weakness and ask him in all humility to fill it with his strength. What an incredible thought: The power that runs the universe is available to me if I am humble enough to accept it.

How do I experience that power? It depends on the situation.

First, God gives me strength to keep going during those times—like that memorable holiday seminar—when my strength gives out. This is almost like spiritual first aid. God may have a lesson for me to learn in the incident, or he may be telling me I need to slow down or make a change. But in the meantime, he often lends me an infusion of strength to carry me through.

Often the strength comes through other people. Ellen was God's strength to me in these awful moments before the holiday seminar. And my Bob has consistently been a source of strength to me in the course of our life together. I especially appreciate his strength and support after I've been on the platform all day and given out everything I know to give. When I feel that all my energy has been drained from my cup, that my strength is totally depleted, Bob will step in to pack up the materials and load the van and take me to dinner. Often he'll carry the conversation or just sit in silence because he understands that I'm all "talked out."

Bob does so much for me that I've always thought of him as "the strong one." But I've begun to realize that Bob and I take turns being strong for each other.

I've seen this with special clarity in the past few years, as we have struggled to cope with painful events in our family. We have rarely been weak at the same time. When Bob is really upset and doesn't feel he can tolerate what's going on, I seem to be handling the situation better or praying more consistently or keeping on a more even keel. Then, when I've had all I can take, Bob will be holding steady.

This is a natural rhythm. I've seen it work with employees in a business and with children in a family. And it works with non-Christians as well as Christians. But I think it is a rhythm God uses to help us. We take turns being God's strength to one another as we care for the people we love.

But God doesn't just work through loved ones in providing the infusions of strength I need to move forward. I've found he can be amazingly creative in supplying me with strength I need. I've had acquaintances or even strangers call me and say, "I'm not sure why I'm calling you, but I want you to know I'm praying for you." Sometimes when that has happened I hadn't even realized I had a need! But other times I knew exactly what the problem was. What a blessing to hear over the phone, “I don’t need to know what you’re going through; I just really feel that you need some strength from me.”

But God’s strength is not available just for crisis times. It is also available for my everyday life, for those ordinary days and weeks when nothing much seems to be happening. In those times I need strength to honor my commitments, to do what I ought to do, to keep from being worn down in the daily grind.

This kind of strength comes to me most dependably in my daily communion with God. When I am spending time in the Word and leaning on him in daily prayer, I am also growing stronger. Not only am I better able to handle my ordinary life today, I am also better equipped for tomorrow’s crisis.

I find it works a little like that wonderful fabric stiffener you can buy in craft stores. The stiffener is used for making fabric bows that hold their shape without wilting—wonderful for decorating baskets and floral arrangements. To make a bow, you take a strip of fabric and soak it in the thick liquid until all the fibers have been permeated. Then you shape the bow and allow it to dry. The finished product is sturdy and flexible; bows made through this process are beautiful and shapely, and they don’t sag or fray.

My times of communion with God work like that stiffener in my life. They soak the fibers of my being in the Lord's strength. When I spend time in prayer and meditation, when I read his Word or read what others have written about him, when I sing or praise or just try to spend time in his presence, I am soaking him up. In myself, I'm still that limp old cotton fabric. But when I have been permeated by him I have the capacity to be strong and resilient and beautiful.

But there's more to living in the Lord's strength than just "soaking" in Scripture and prayer. The actual process of becoming strong and beautiful takes a bit more energy. Growing strong in the Lord is not usually just a matter of sitting around and waiting until I'm strong so that *then* I can do what he wants me to do. More often, it's a matter of doing what I think God wants me to do, trusting that I will be given the strength I need when I need it.

In other words, God doesn't expect me to be strong.

But he does expect me to be obedient.

And I have to say yes to his leading if I want to be a strong woman of God.

I have to follow up on the little nudges and the big messages he has sent me in my prayer times and during the day. I have to step forward, trusting that the

Lord who gave the orders will also provide the strength to carry them out.

And that, in turn, takes courage.

It takes courage to say yes to being weak, courage to say yes to the Lord's leading instead of depending on your own strength, courage to say, "I can't do it, Lord. But I'll still try if you go with me."

I have learned that the most amazing infusions of God's strength happen like that, when I am taking the risk of obeying God. So often in my life I have been astonished at how my Lord can take a tiny faith step and turn it into a strong leap for his kingdom.

It's a little like those moving sidewalks in a big airport.

These days, it seems that Bob and I spend half our lives in airports, so we loved this image, which came from my friend Anne's prayer group. (One of the group members even wrote a country-western song about it!)

Picture yourself walking down the concourse, lugging your shoulder bags and dragging your rolling cart behind you. Your boss has sent you on a special assignment, and your gate is at the very end of an impossibly long corridor. But just up ahead you spot the long black walkway with the handrails. It's the moving sidewalk.

A woman just a few paces ahead of you steps on. She's obviously very weak and weary, so she just grabs onto the handrail and lets the walkway carry her along.

Right after her is a businessman with no luggage but a briefcase. He's obviously not in a hurry. So he just steps onto the sidewalk and moves along at a regular pace. But the momentum of the moving panel does add an extra bounce to his step. You can tell because he's passing the people who decided not to take the walkway.

You don't have the leisure of a stroll down the concourse. You have a mission to accomplish, and you're already walking as fast as you can. Without slowing your pace, you take a big step onto the walkway. And whoosh! you feel the power. Now every step feels like a giant step, taken with less effort. You feel like you're in an old-fashioned sneaker commercial, running faster and jumping higher. The steps are yours, but the walkway is carrying you, too.

I often have that "whoosh" feeling when I step on a platform to speak. I am always in awe of the responsibility I have to the women in my audiences. And there are times when I am so weak, when I feel I don't have the energy to connect even with God. But I am convinced that this is where God wants me, so I go ahead and step on the platform. And in a matter of moments the Spirit of God will take over and strengthen me and give me the power I need to share myself and my Lord.

It doesn't always happen that way. Sometimes I feel pretty energetic and strong, and I may decide to go it on my own. I may decide to skip the moving sidewalk and just walk down the concourse myself. And sometimes I guess I do a pretty good job that way. But it's completely different when I'm relying on the Lord's strength, depending on him to do what needs to be done. I can almost feel the moment when I lean on the Lord and let his strength take over. Whoosh!

And although I've seen it again and again, I'm always amazed at what happens next. I will look out and see every eye glued on me, every ear tuned to the words coming out of my mouth. Sometimes I'll see tears running down cheeks. And then I'll think, "But this is just me—an ordinary housewife and mother with a high school education and a dysfunctional background and no training in speaking or writing. What am I doing here that would be so meaningful to them?"

I really am not trying to put myself down here. I know that God has made me special. But I also know that what happens in those seminars is so far beyond what I am capable of on my own that I can't take any of the credit. It's God's strength and the power of his Word coming through.

And that power and strength is available to you, no matter what your life is like, whether you're at the end of your rope or just moving along in an ordinary life or ready to take a big, risky step into ministry of some kind. The promise of God's strength doesn't apply just to speakers or writers or ministers. I have seen him at work in so many different lives, seen the amazing things that result when men and women give him their weakness and rely on his strength.

I think of a woman I know who has suffered emotional problems to the point of being in and out of mental hospitals. I can't imagine coping with the kind of pain she has endured. And yet she keeps moving forward, keeps holding out her cup to receive the Lord's strength. She uplifts me.

Or I think of friend whose only daughter has struggled with dyslexia, has had an abortion, has attempted suicide. My friend has agonized, worried, intervened. She has also had to cope with losing a house and with ongoing financial instability. Yet this is the friend who has taught me how to crawl up into the lap of my heavenly Father and find strength in his arms. She teaches me how to find strength in weakness.

I think of my strong Bob, who touches the lives of so many women in our seminars because he is willing to be open and vulnerable to them, to be honest about his feelings and weaknesses. He even lets me talk about him in my seminars—a position of weakness that requires enormous strength and courage. I have always loved and respected my Bob, but my respect has grown as I have observed his willingness to be weak in the Lord's service and have watched him grow stronger in the Lord's love.

I think of so many other people—young moms with children at home, dads whose teenagers are in trouble, people struggling with illness or working at jobs that sap their spirits. And these men and women are an example to me because I see them turning to the Lord in their pain and weakness. Turning to him when life seems too much or just too daily, or when the challenge is beyond them.

The simple child's song really is true.

We *are* weak.

But he *is* strong.

And his mighty arms are outstretched to us, ready to pour out his strength into our weak and fragile little cups.

And all we have to do is hold them up to him.

Savoring God's Word . . .
A Taste of Strength

The Lord is my light and my salvation;
Whom shall I fear?
The Lord is the strength of my life;
Of whom shall I be afraid? . . .
Wait on the Lord;
Be of good courage,
And He shall strengthen your heart;
Wait, I say, on the Lord!

Psalm 27:1, 14

Blessed is the man whose strength is in You, whose heart is set on pilgrimage.

Psalm 84:5

He gives power to the weak, and to those who have no might He increases strength. . . . But those who wait on the Lord shall renew their strength; they shall mount up with wings like eagles, they shall run and not be weary, they shall walk and not faint.

Isaiah 40:29, 31

I have prayed for you, that your faith should not fail; and when you have returned to Me, strengthen your brethren.

Luke 22:32

The foolishness of God is wiser than men, and the weakness of God is stronger than men. For you see your calling, brethren, that not many wise according to the flesh, not many mighty, not many noble, are called. But God has chosen the foolish things of the world to put to shame the wise, and God has chosen the weak things of the world to put to shame the things which are mighty; and the base things of the world and the things which are despised God has chosen, and the things which are not, to bring to nothing the things that are, that no flesh should glory in his presence.

I Corinthians 1:25-29

And He said to me, "My grace is sufficient for you, for My strength is made perfect in weakness." Therefore most gladly I will rather boast in my infirmities, that the power of Christ may rest upon me.

2 Corinthians 12:9

May the God of all grace, who called us to His eternal glory by Christ Jesus, after you have suffered a while, perfect, establish, strengthen, and settle you.

I Peter 5:10

Fill my cup, Lord . . .

I offer my cup of pain—

the cup you know too well.

Fill my cup with thanksgiving and hope

that someday my cup of tears

will be filled with joy.

7

A Cup of Thanksgiving

You prepare a table before me
in the presence of my enemies;
You anoint my head with oil;
my cup runs over.
Psalm 23:5

"For what we are about to receive, the Lord make us truly thankful."

It's a familiar table grace—at least for those of us who still gather around the table at mealtimes and ask a blessing. We say it almost without thinking. It's just one of those standard mealtime prayers—easy to pronounce over a groaning holiday table when loved ones are gathered together.

But have you ever thought of praying that blessing for all the circumstances of your life? Have you ever thought of asking the Lord to give you the gift of gratitude for whatever life has poured into your cup?

That's what I'm trying to learn.

These days I am trying to pray this way on a daily basis.

"Lord, for *whatever* I am receiving and about to receive—pain as well as joy—please teach me the secret of giving thanks. For what I have already received—what has shaped my life in the past, and what is shaping me today—please fill my cup with thankfulness."

This is not an easy prayer to say with sincerity. In fact, I often feel a little hypocritical when I'm praying it. There are quite a few times in my life when I don't really *want* to be thankful.

I'm not particularly inclined to be thankful when there is upset and pain in our family. I don't really feel thankful for the chronic pain that some of my friends are suffering in their bodies. I'm certainly not up to offering a heartfelt thanksgiving when I feel like the world and even God have slapped me in the face.

Yes, I know we are supposed to "rejoice always, pray without ceasing, in everything give thanks" (1 Thessalonians 5:16-18). I believe that. But how often do the thank-yous come through gritted teeth? How often have I had to offer thanks because God said so, all the while feeling like a liar?

It's one thing to offer thanks because it's the right thing to do.

It's another thing to be truly thankful.

So how do I do it?

Only by remembering that all things come from God, including our own attitudes. An attitude of thankfulness is a gift God gives to us, a healing libation he pours into our cups. But we must choose to accept it, even to ask for it. Our part is to offer whatever is in our cup to the Lord, and then ask him to fill our cup with true thankfulness.

"For what I am about to receive, the Lord make me truly thankful."

What I am asking for, really, is an attitude adjustment. I am asking for a new way of looking at my life—past, present, and future.

Filling my cup with thankfulness for the past, for instance, means taking a step beyond forgiveness and opening my arms to the circumstances that made me what I am today. It means developing a new attitude toward the people and events that influenced me, even those who treated me ill or meant me harm. It means celebrating the good that God was able to do through those circumstances.

Yes, it's hard, especially for those of us whose childhoods were painful. For a few, filling our cup with gratitude for the past means just being grateful that it's over! But most of us who hold our cup of past pain up to the Lord will find that a thankful attitude can transform even painful memories.

I am finally reaching a place, for example, where I can honestly thank God for my father and even for the turmoil I experienced while growing up—not because that turmoil was part of God's plan, but because as I look back I can see God working in the midst of it all. As my attitude adjusts into a spirit of thanksgiving, I am able to see beautiful tracings of God's handiwork in my dark memories. For it was the turmoil and insecurity I knew in those days that made me so hungry to know a Father God, that gave me such a yearning for a Savior. Had my Jewish upbringing been happier or more secure, perhaps I would not have embraced the Messiah.

There are many other difficult areas of my past that I am learning to embrace, to see with eyes of gratitude. There may be painful things in your past, too, that need to be redeemed with the eyes of thanksgiving. Or perhaps there are hidden treasures, unappreciated legacies that begin to gleam when viewed in a thankful light.

I'm always amazed, for instance, when women complain to me that they "don't have a testimony" because they grew up in a Christian home. They seem sad or a little embarrassed that they don't have a dramatic story to tell of a radical life-change. It's as if they think they have somehow been robbed of the ability to have an influence for the Lord.

What a devious ploy of Satan—to turn a magnificent, gracious gift into a source of embarrassment! Being raised in a Christian home is a reason for profuse thanksgiving. Scripture, hymns, and Christian attitudes learned early become a fountain of enrichment for all of life. I have to really praise our grandchildren's parents for a good Christian foundation in their school and church. Tears fill my eyes when I see them praying or studying Scripture because I never had that kind of solid spiritual grounding in my young life. Whether or not God gives those children a dramatic "testimony," they will always have the Word of God deep in their hearts. That is good reason to be truly thankful.

But the attitude adjustment of thanksgiving is not just for the past. It's something I need every day in the present, and for the future.

To fill my present cup with thanksgiving means to live in the belief that God is working for good even when things seem to be falling apart.

And I find that harder to do right now than I have at any other time in my life.

The last few years have been difficult ones for our family. I have found it harder to trust God, harder to speak with confidence, harder sometimes even to get through the day. Harder, certainly, to live in thanksgiving. Day to day, my cup has been filled with pain.

And yet that is exactly why I so desperately need the attitude adjustment of thanksgiving. I need it to give meaning to my pain, to redeem it with the reminder of what God has to offer me in my hurtful circumstances.

And what does God give me in my pain? What reason do I have to be thankful?

First of all, he offers the gift of comfort—a significant mercy.

The promise is stark and direct in the King James version: "I will not leave you comfortless" (John 14:18). Other translations say it differently: "I will not leave you all alone" (TEV), "I will not leave you desolate" (RSV), "I will not leave you as orphans" (NIV). But the message is the same.

You may be hurting, says the Lord, but I will be with you all along the way. If you trust me, I will provide you comfort.

I have been comforted profoundly at times, in the very center of my pain, by a simple sense of God's presence, the nearness of the Holy Spirit. I can come to him and simply lean on him, drawing comfort from his nearness. Sometimes I pray, sharing my troubles and asking for his help. Or sometimes my knees buckle and I sink down wordless in the arms of my heavenly Father. If I pray on a disciplined, consistent basis, my prayer closet is likely the first place I want to go when my cup fills with pain.

And yet there are other times when I need the Lord's comfort in more concrete form. Especially during those times when my faith is weak or my spirit is overwhelmed or my body is failing me, I need God's presence to be incarnated—to take on flesh. And in those times he brings me comfort in the form of friends who love me and pray for me or simply watch and wait with me.

I will never forget the comfort a friend offered to me in Jesus' name during a time of awful physical pain. I learned later that I had picked up a parasite in my colon. But at the time I knew only that something was making my abdomen hurt. The pain quickly became so bad that I had to excuse myself from a dinner party and lie down. I lay there ten or fifteen minutes, curled up in a fetal position, fearful and hurting. And then my friend Susan came in. She put her arms around me and prayed for me, and I felt that God had sent an angel to comfort me. The pain didn't stop or go away, but it became tolerable. I was able to go home and sleep, and the next day I went to the doctor.

A special source of comfort in times of pain is the companionship of those who have been through the same ordeal. There is a sense of camaraderie and understanding in shared pain, and I believe God uses that fellowship to extend comfort to his children.

Several years ago I broke my foot. I quickly found that while many people were sympathetic, those who had been through the same experience could offer a special kind of comfort because they really understood what I was facing. And now, whenever I see someone with a cast, my empathy and compassion begin to flow. I can honestly say, "I know exactly how that feels, how that pain can shoot, how that foot burns." In the same way, I can resonate with the pain of those who have lost a parent or who have grown up in an alcoholic home. I can offer them a special brand of comfort because I *know.* I understand.

That doesn't mean, of course, that I can't offer comfort to someone who is going through something I haven't experienced. If I am willing, God can work through me to extend his comfort to anyone in pain, just as he works through others to comfort me. I can offer my presence, my words. I can bring a casserole or volunteer to help with chores. I can offer myself to the Lord as a human expression of his comfort. And I know that he works through such an offering, because I have been on the receiving end. I have been deeply comforted by men and women who showed me the Lord's comfort.

For the Christian there's probably not much else that comforts the soul more than God's Word. I find the psalms especially helpful. They are so honest and direct. They remind me that I am not alone in my pain, and they carry me through my pain to renewed faith. They help me adjust my attitude to one of thanksgiving.

But the most compelling source of comfort I find in Scripture is the reminder that my Lord is no stranger to pain. He chose to become human, to share our pain in order to move us beyond it. He knows what it is like to be rejected, to feel physical discomfort and spiritual desolation, to pray that the cup of pain would be taken away. He knows what agony is like, even what death is like.

But there is more than companionship here. I learn this, too, in the pages of holy Scripture.

My Lord is with me in my pain, but he also is greater than pain, greater than fear, greater even than death. He is with me in the midst of my suffering, but he will also carry me beyond it. If I continue holding up my cup to him, he will do more than fill it, he will also transform it.

This promise of transformation is the second gift our Lord has to offer in my pain. And this is not a consolation prize. This is not a paltry offering I get in return for giving up on earthly happiness. What God promises me in the midst of my pain is real life, real joy, incredible growth, unbelievable beauty.

This is what God has had in mind for me all along. This is what he is doing in the midst of all my circumstances. In the long run, this is "what I am about to receive." I'm going to be changed into something wonderful.

Because I love to collect beautiful teacups and saucers, I love a little parable someone shared with me years ago. I have taken this little tale by an unknown author and retold it in a way that speaks most deeply to me about my own pain and my own transformation.

The story begins in a little gift shop, a charming establishment crammed full of delightful discoveries. A man and a woman have gone there to find a special gift for their granddaughter's birthday. With excited oohs and ahs, they pick up dolls and books and figurines, intent on finding just the perfect piece.

Suddenly, glancing into the corner of an antique armoire, the grandmother spies a prize.

"Oh, honey, look!" she exclaims, taking him by the arm and pointing. Carefully he reaches over to pick up the delicate teacup in his big hand. A shaft of sunlight from the window shines through the translucent china, illuminating a delicate design.

"Oh, isn't it pretty?" the grandmother sighs.

He nods, "I don't know much about dishes, but I'd have to say that's the best-looking cup I've ever seen."

Together they gaze at the beautiful little cup, already imagining their granddaughter's face when she opens her special gift. And at that moment something remarkable happens. Something magic.

With a voice as clear and sweet as the painted nosegay on the saucer, that teacup begins to talk.

"I thank you for the compliment," the cup begins. "But you know, I haven't always been like this."

A little shaken at being addressed by a teacup, the grandfather places it back on the shelf and takes a step back. But his wife doesn't seem surprised at all. Instead, she asks with interest, "Whatever are you talking about?"

"Well," says the teacup, "I wasn't always beautiful. In fact, I started out as an ugly, soggy lump of clay. But one day a man with dirty, wet hands started slinging me around, pounding me on a worktable, knocking the breath out of me. I didn't like this procedure one little bit. It hurt, and it made me angry.

"Stop!" I cried.

"But the man with the wet hands simply said, 'Not yet!'

"Finally the pounding stopped, and I breathed a sigh of relief. I thought my ordeal was over. But it had just begun.

"The next thing I knew, I was being stuffed into a mold—packed in so tightly I couldn't see straight.

" 'Stop! Stop!' I cried until I was squeezed too tight to utter a sound. Parts of me oozed out of the mold, and he scraped these away.

"If I could have talked, I would have screamed.

"But the man seemed to know what I was thinking. He just looked down with a patient expression on his face and told me, 'Not yet.'

"Finally, the pressing and the scraping stopped. But the next experience was far worse. I was plunged into the dark, and then the temperature began to rise. The air grew hotter and hotter, until I was in agony. I still couldn't talk, but inside I was yelling, 'Get me out of here!'

"And strangely, through those thick furnace walls, I seemed to hear someone saying, 'Not yet.'

"Just when I was sure I was going to be completely incinerated, the oven began to cool. Eventually the man took me out of the furnace and released me from that confining mold. I relaxed. I even looked around and enjoyed my new form. I was firmer. I had shape. This was better.

"But then came the short lady in the smock. She pulled out tiny brushes and began to daub paint all over me. The fumes made me feel sick, and the brush tickled.

" 'I don't like that.' I cried. 'I've had enough. Please stop.'

" 'Not yet!' said the short lady with a smile.

"Finally she finished. She picked up her brushes and moved on. But just when I thought I was finally free, the first man picked me up again and put me back into that awful furnace. This time was worse than before because I wasn't protected by the mold.

"Again and again I screamed, 'Stop!'

"And each time the man answered through the door of the furnace, 'Not yet!'

"Finally the oven cooled once more, and the man came to open the door. By that time I was almost done in. I barely noticed when I was picked up and put down and packed in a box and jounced and jolted some more. When I finally came to, a pretty lady was picking me up out of my box and placing me on this shelf, next to this mirror.

"And when I looked at myself in the mirror, I was amazed. No longer was I ugly, soggy, and dirty. I was shining and clean. And I was beautiful—unbelievably beautiful. 'Could this be me?' I cried for joy.

"It was then" said the teacup, "that I realized there was a purpose in all that pain. You see, it took all that suffering to make me truly beautiful."

And we can be beautiful, too. That's what God wants for us regardless of the circumstances of our lives.

That doesn't mean that God sends us pain just to test us. I don't believe that God kills off loved ones and tortures innocent children with incurable diseases and turns our friends against us just so that he can teach us a lesson. The God of the New Testament is not a sadistic deity who delights in sending trials just to see if we humans will make it through. He doesn't have to. The human race and the forces of darkness are quite up to the challenge of causing enough pain and suffering and rejection to go around.

And yet our God, through his magnificent powers of redemption, has never lost the upper hand. Whatever ugliness we encounter, whatever suffering we undergo, whatever pain we stumble through, he has the power to redeem it, if we continue to hold up our cups to him.

We can take the pain of our past and the pain of our present and allow that pain to encase us for a lifetime if we want to. But that isn't what God wants us to do. God wants us to bring our cup of pain to him. He wants to comfort us, and he wants to transform us into something beautiful.

And for his loving presence yesterday and today and tomorrow, we can be truly and sincerely thankful.

Savoring God's Word . . . A Taste of Thankfulness

Sing praise to the Lord,
You saints of His,
And give thanks at the remembrance of His holy name.
For His anger is but for a moment,
His favor is for life;
Weeping may endure for a night,
But joy comes in the morning. . . .
Hear, O Lord, and have mercy on me;
Lord, be my helper!
You have turned for me my mourning into dancing;
You have put off my sackcloth and clothed me with gladness,
To the end that my glory may sing praise to You and not be silent.
O Lord my God, I will give thanks to You forever.

Psalm 30:4,5,10-12

Those who sow in tears
Shall reap in joy.
He who continually goes forth weeping,
Bearing seed for sowing,
Shall doubtless come again with rejoicing,
Bringing his sheaves with him.

Psalm 126:5,6

We do not have a High Priest who cannot sympathize with our weaknesses, but was in all points tempted as we are, yet without sin. Let us therefore come boldly to the throne of grace, that we may obtain mercy and find grace to help in time of need.

Hebrews 4:15,16

In this you greatly rejoice, though now for a little while, if need be, you have been grieved by various trials, that the genuineness of your faith, being much more precious than gold that perishes, though it is tested by fire, may be found to praise, honor, and glory at the revelation of Jesus Christ, whom having not seen you love. Though now you do not see Him, yet believing you rejoice with joy inexplicable and full of glory, receiving the end of your faith—the salvation of your souls. . . . Therefore gird up the loins of your mind, be sober, and rest your hope fully upon the grace that is to be brought to you at the revelation of Jesus Christ.

I Peter 1:6-9,13

Rejoice always, pray without ceasing, in everything give thanks; for this is the will of God in Christ Jesus for you.

I Thessalonians 5:16-18

Fill my cup, Lord . . .

I surrender my cup to you,

that you may fill it with service

and the sweetness

of your presence.

8

A Cup of Service

Surely goodness and mercy
shall follow me all the days of my life;
and I will dwell in the
house of the Lord forever.
Psalm 23:6

It's such a simple, beautiful process.

I hold up my cup to my loving, giving heavenly Father.

He cleanses me of the old, the impure, the bitter—empties my cup and wipes it clean. Then he fills my cup with living water—fills it with quietness, with encouragement and forgiveness, with trust and communion and strength and thanksgiving.

His blessings flow. My cup overflows.

But there is a catch.

Or rather, there is a requirement.

The Lord's blessings flow freely, but receiving them in my life involves two important acts on my part.

First, I surrender.

Second, I serve.

Surrender is the very act of holding up my cup, handing my life over to him. My Lord Jesus supplies everything I need in my life, but he also demands everything. He asks for the whole of my life—my heart and my soul and my mind.

Sometimes it feels like a blessed relief, sometimes a painful sacrifice, often a mixture of the two. But it's never, ever a bad bargain.

I give him all I can of me.

He fills me with all I could ever want of him. And then he gives me back myself as well.

I've learned this dramatic lesson about submission over and over in my life, but two instances stand out in my memory.

The first surrender came when I gave my life to Christ. That was a big step for a Jewish teenager from a dysfunctional family. Most of my relatives thought I was crazy; they were sure I was making the biggest mistake of my life. Or perhaps they thought I was just converting so I could be with Bob. Several predicted we would never last.

But my surrender to the Lord Jesus Christ at the age of sixteen was real, and it changed everything. I came to Jesus with my whole heart, held out the cup of my life to him, and he filled it with himself. In the years that followed, he honored my submission by continuing to fill my cup with blessings. I grew. I learned. I made plenty of mistakes and felt my share of pain. But I never doubted my decision to submit my life to Jesus Christ, the Messiah.

Many years later came a second surrender that was both quieter and more earthshaking. It happened about the time that our daughter Jenny was leaving for college.

I remember the day so clearly. Jenny had been packing for days, and now she was actually loading her little Volkswagen convertible with everything she needed in her dorm room—her clothes and her cheerleading stool and her teddy bears and her plants and her pillows. I helped her make trip after trip from the house to the car. And all the while I was thinking, *Well, this is it. This is the day we've been waiting for.*

You see, Bob and I had planned our lives carefully. We had decided to have our children while we were young so that when we reached our forties our children would be out of the nest and we would have each other again. So I was very excited as I watched Jenny drive down the hill in her little blue bug. I followed her down the driveway waving and blowing kisses. I watched that little car disappear around the corner. And then I headed back to the house, thinking, *Wow, this is great. No more kids, no more running in and out. No more mess and loud music and food all over the place and worrying about where everybody is. Now I've finally got my life back.*

I walked into the front foyer and just stood there breathing in the peace and quiet. Everything looked just perfect. Every picture on every wall was straight and dusted. Every knick-knack was in place.

I walked down the hall to Jenny's room, half expecting it to be a mess from all her packing. But it was perfect; she had left everything in order. *Well, Mom,* I thought, *you've trained her really well.*

I stepped into Brad's room—he'd been away a few years. Everything was perfect there, too. All his trophies and memorabilia were lined up neatly on the shelves, and his bedspread was perfectly smooth. Without thinking I reached out to straighten a book on the shelf, but it didn't really need straightening.

I walked back down the hall, thinking again that everything looked just perfect. The house was so quiet that I could hear myself breathe.

At that time Bob owned a mobile home company. The business was struggling, so Bob was putting in a lot of extra hours. I knew he wouldn't be home until very late.

And now I found myself thinking, *You know, my children don't really need me anymore. They've got lives of their own now.*

And I thought, *My husband doesn't really need me because he's working late and he's putting all his time and energy into his business.*

And I looked around my shining, perfect kitchen and I thought, *My house doesn't even need me. I can whip it into shape in just fifteen minutes a day.*

All of a sudden the loneliness and the confusion hit me like a blow to the stomach. *Who am I now? What is there left for me to do?*

I went into the bedroom, where I usually had my prayer time. Everything looked perfect there, too, but I didn't notice. I didn't even get down on my knees like I usually did to pray. I just slumped down on the floor and cried, "God, I don't understand this. Why am I feeling so awful? This should be the most wonderful day of my life."

And it was that very day, down on that perfectly vacuumed floor, that I surrendered again.

I said, "God, you can do anything you want with me. I'm yours. I submit myself to you today."

I had no idea then what would happen. But God knew. He was already in the process of putting together the events that would launch my life in a direction that still astounds me.

You see, right about this time, I was reluctantly in the process of becoming an author. For several years I had been speaking to women's groups about home management, and my friend and mentor Florence Littauer had been after me to write a book. "I can't write," I had told her again and again. So finally her publisher had arranged to turn some of my speaking tapes into a book called *More Hours in My Day.* I received my first copies a few months after God and I had that session on my bedroom floor.

Meanwhile, Bob had finally decided to pull the plug on his struggling business. He sold the mobile home company and began looking for something else to do. But when I was invited to promote my book on a radio talk show in Los Angeles, Bob said he was free to drive me into town.

It was supposed to be a twenty-minute interview. Rich Buhler, the host, talked to us briefly beforehand and told us what to expect. "We'll talk about your book for ten minutes, and then we'll put you on the phone lines for ten minutes so you can answer questions for any people who may call in."

That sounded all right to me. I was too dazed at the idea of being an author to have any real opinions, anyway. So we began the interview, and suddenly the phones begin lighting up like crazy. I answered question after question, and the call-in lights were still blinking when my ten minutes were up. "I've never had this kind of response to a call-in show," Rich said. "Do you think you can stay a little bit longer?"

I looked at Bob, and he nodded. After all, we were in downtown Los Angeles at four o'clock in the afternoon, and who wants to get on a freeway in downtown Los Angeles at four o'clock in the afternoon? "We can stay," I told Rich.

That twenty-minute interview turned into a three-and-a-half hour marathon. And we got home to find the answering machine light blinking furiously and the answering machine tape completely used up. More than forty-five calls had come in—all in response to that radio interview.

The next day I was slated to speak at a mother-daughter tea. Bob told me, "Honey, I'm going to be home tomorrow, so I'll call all these people back." But he didn't. In fact, when I came home the following afternoon he was so hoarse he could barely talk.

"You wouldn't believe what's gone on today!" he croaked. "I couldn't even get started on returning the messages because the phone has been ringing all day."

"I have prayed with women on the phone," he said. "I've given them household hints. And Emilie, don't get excited, but I have just booked you to speak in thirty-eight churches!"

I couldn't even speak. I just stared at him. All this was beyond my comprehension.

"I'll carry your books for you when you speak," Bob went on. "And when the phone stops ringing, then I'll go out and get a regular job."

That was fifteen years ago. Bob is still carrying my books, and doing so much more. Between us, we have written almost two dozen books, and we have done seminars across the United States and Canada. We have met and served with some of the great Christian communicators of our day. We have been received into the hearts of thousands of dear Christian men and women.

And what truly overwhelms me about it all is that I never set out to do any of this. I never planned to write books or have a ministry. Neither did Bob.

What we did do was surrender. We held up our cups to the Lord and poured out our own agenda and asked him to fill our cups with what he wanted for us. He did. And the results still leave me openmouthed. I can't believe it's me doing all this. But it is. In a way, I feel like I'm more "me" than ever. My life is richer, more exciting. I know I'm where God wants me to be right now.

And that's what surrender can do.

But a second thing is required of me in this beautiful process of having my cup filled.

The stream of living water is supposed to keep on flowing. It's not supposed to stop with me. Blessings stagnate when they remain in my cup. I need to pass them on to others through service.

And what is service? Service is honoring the Lord by doing what he has told us to do. And what he has told us to do is to love him first and then to love others as much as we love ourselves.

That's why true service and surrender always go together.

In order to truly serve, I have to surrender my right to have my own way, my right to put my own comfort first. In return, I experience the joy of giving, of being a conduit of God's blessing. And this is truly a great joy.

Yet the cup of service can be an acquired taste, like rich espresso or caviar. For most of us humans, service doesn't come naturally. We like having our needs catered to. We like being taken care of. We like being served more than we like serving. And if we do serve others, we typically expect something in return. We scratch a back in hopes of having our own scratched. Or we offer good deeds in the hopes of improving our own reputation or just to make ourselves feel virtuous. Selfishness and power games come far more naturally to most of us than true, loving service.

And that again is why surrender has to come first. We develop a taste for service only as we develop a taste for Jesus—as we learn from him and know what it is like to have our cup filled with his blessings. We learn it from his example, and from the example of others who do his will. And we learn to serve others as we learn to serve him. It all goes together. It's hard to have one without the other.

The good news is that our motives don't have to be unmixed before we can begin the act of serving others. We don't even have to be living in perfect surrender to Jesus. (How many of us manage to live in perfect surrender all of the time anyway?)

The beauty of living in Christ is that he can use us in his service just as we are. He can redeem our blundering efforts—and his living water sparkles just as brightly when served in our cracked cups.

That said, how do we actually go about serving the Lord and serving others?

One way to serve is through vocation, through doing the work God calls you to do. This may be what you do for a living or what you do as a volunteer. But if you can't find any way to serve God and your fellow humans through the work that you do, you need to find another line of work!

Bob and I feel enormously blessed that we are able to make our living in direct ministry, speaking and writing about the Lord. Yet a job doesn't have to be inherently "Christian" to offer opportunities for Christian service. You can wait tables for the Lord, treating your customers with respect and kindness. You can paint houses for the Lord, conducting your business fairly and praying for the occupants of the houses you paint. And you can certainly raise children for the Lord, because everything you do and say will make an impression on those little ones.

Another way I serve Jesus and others is through prayer. We all need to be filling our cup daily with prayer for friends, for those in authority, for our churches and our families, and for our children—especially for our children, because the only assurance we have of access to our children's hearts is through prayer and the power of the Holy Spirit. We need to pray for wisdom, pray for understanding, pray that they will grow up loving and fearing the Lord.

Prayer can be a form of service in itself, but it also increases our capacity and desire to serve in other ways. When I am coming to the Lord regularly in prayer, I am usually growing in compassion, growing in understanding, growing in my willingness to serve.

This aspect of prayer has made a big impression on me during the past year. I have fervently prayed for someone I love, someone I felt was making a series of wrong decisions. And as I have prayed, I have been reminded that while my prayer changes a lot of things, it changes *me* most of all. I just knew that if I prayed hard enough, this person would eventually change her mind and do what I thought she should do. What has happened, instead, is that I have gradually been able to turn her over to God. Now, instead of praying that she will follow a certain path, I find myself praying that whatever path she takes will bring her closer to God.

In the meantime, as I have prayed, I have also drawn closer to my heavenly Father. Gently he has shown me ways that I can truly serve this precious person without pushing my own agenda on her. Gently he has led me toward caring for her more unselfishly.

And caring is yet another important form of service. I serve God and others when I notice their needs and act in ways that will help them.

More than once I have learned lessons in that kind of caring from our children and grandchildren. Our daughter Jenny, who worked as a waitress when she was younger, has fine-tuned those beautiful waitress skills of serving others and making them feel cared for. I love to watch her when she entertains, noticing the needs of her family and guests and deftly tending to them.

Our son Brad, too, moves me to admiration with his sensitive spirit and servant's heart. I remember especially the way he served my mother, his grandmother, when she was growing older. We were a busy, bustling, fast-moving family. Grandma Irene couldn't move very fast. And Brad was always the one who would wait for her, take her arm, help her out of the car, and walk slowly so she could keep up. He served her in a beautiful way, and as a result they developed a special relationship.

Our little grandson Chad gave us another eloquent lesson in caring a couple of years ago when our whole family took a vacation in Mexico. We were shopping in the little town near our resort, and Chad spotted a woman with a tiny baby sitting on the sidewalk, begging. We had told the children that people might ask them for money and that they might want to give a little. But we were surprised when Chad pulled a five-dollar bill out of his pocket and gave it to the woman.

"Wow, Chad," said his big sister, Christine. "You gave her all your spending money."

He shrugged. "She needed it more than I did," he told us nonchalantly.

And tears came to my eyes at this beautiful example of caring and service. Chad wasn't responding to guilt or pressure. He saw the woman's need, he cared, and he did what he could to help her. That's true service.

I serve God and others when I notice people's needs and care about them and respond to them. But there is yet another way to serve. It is obvious enough to sound silly, but it's a challenge for many people.

Simply put, I serve through serving!

That is, I serve by performing the kind of ordinary, menial tasks that meet needs but seldom bring recognition and glory. Service can be scrubbing a toilet, cooking a meal, taking an elderly neighbor to the grocery store. Any of these humble chores, when done in Jesus' name, can be a graceful dance of love. In fact, this kind of mundane chore seems to have a special power to communicate the Lord's love. Surely that is why Jesus singled out this kind of service—feeding the hungry, visiting the prisoners, ministering to the sick—and stressed, "Inasmuch as you did it to one of the least of these My brethren, you did it to Me."

I hope I'm learning to do that. I hope I'm learning to hold up my cup to my Lord in surrender and get it filled with his love, then pour the love out in service to those around me. I want to be a better servant to the people who read my books and come to my seminars, to the people I worship with at church, to the people I encounter at the supermarket. And I want to be a better servant to my own family—these people I love the most are sometimes the most difficult for me to serve.

Every Christmas, Bob and I invite my entire extended family over for a holiday dinner. And you have to understand that this is not a typical Norman Rockwell scene. Many people attend my seminars and read my books and just assume that my life is perfect—beautiful home, loving family, adorable kids, all clean and shining and organized. But let me tell you a little about the people who sit around my table at Christmas dinner.

We have a doctor and a dentist, the president of a large shoe company, an attorney, and several educators. We also have a bartender, a masseuse, and several who are unemployed. A few of us are homeless or near homeless. One is homosexual, another is HIV positive, yet another is involved with New Age practice. There is an ex-convict, more than one person with chemical dependencies (some recovering), several children who were drug babies. Some are married, some are single, several are divorced or separated. And all are gathered at the home of their Hebrew Christian sister/aunt/cousin Emilie, whom they are sure is totally weird!

These people are all family to me. God gave me these people to serve, and he wants to pour out his love on them through me. I don't know how well or how unselfishly I carry out this task. We don't have very much in common, and our time together sometimes feels awkward. But when they leave, they always say they had a great time. And I always fill a tote bag of food (turkey to make a sandwich, half a loaf of bread, my ten-bean soup). I feel I fed them and loved them like Jesus would, and that feeling fills my cup to overflowing.

Then there was the year I sat on a stool in the middle of our living room with all these people around me and read *The Story of Three Trees.* Three grandchildren, who were five, seven, and nine at the time, wrapped themselves in blankets and pillowcases and acted out the whole story of the tree that became the manger. This was not a carefully staged pageant. It was an impromptu, volunteer production, a gift of love. And that night when my wide assortment of family left, they all said, "This is the best Christmas we've ever had."

And that's how service works. When the Lord fills our cup, he fills it to be used. He intends for us to fill the cups of others the best way we know how.

And when we do, the sweetness of his love and peace flows from cup . . . to cup . . . to cup . . . to cup.

In his name.

Amen.

Savoring God's Word . . .
A Taste of Service

And now, Israel, what does the Lord your God require of you, but to fear the Lord your God, to walk in all His ways and to love Him, to serve the Lord your God with all your heart and with all your soul.

Deuteronomy 10:12

Then the King will say to those on His right hand, "Come, you blessed of My Father, inherit the kingdom prepared for you from the foundation of the world: for I was hungry and you gave Me food; I was thirsty and you gave Me drink; I was a stranger and you took Me in; I was naked and you clothed Me; I was sick and you visited Me; I was in prison and you came to Me." Then the righteous will answer Him, saying, "Lord, when did we see You hungry and feed You, or thirsty and give You drink? When did we see You a stranger and take You in, or naked and clothe You? Or when did we see You sick, or in prison, and come to You?" And the King will answer and say to them, "Assuredly, I say to you, inasmuch as you did it to one of the least of these My brethren, you did it to Me."

Jesus . . . knowing that the Father had given all things into His hands, and that He had come from God and was going to God, rose from supper and laid aside His garments, took a towel and girded Himself. After that, He poured water into a basin and began to wash the disciples' feet, and to wipe them with the towel with which He was girded. Then He came to Simon Peter. And Peter said to Him, "Lord, are You washing my feet?" Jesus answered and said to him, "What I am doing you do not understand now, but you will know after this." . . . So when He had washed their feet, taken His garments, and sat down again, He said to them, "Do you know what I have done to you? You call Me Teacher and Lord, and you say well, for so I am. If I then, your Lord and Teacher, have washed your feet, you also ought to wash one another's feet. For I have given you an example, that you should do as I have done to you. Most assuredly, I say to you, a servant is not greater than his master; nor is he who is sent greater than he who sent him.

John 13:3-16

Walk in love, as Christ also has loved us and given Himself for us, an offering and a sacrifice to God.

Ephesians 5:2

Fill my cup, Lord . . .

I offer my cup of me,

that it may be filled

to overflowing

with you.

Fill My Cup, Lord . . .

Fill my cup, Lord.
I hold it up to you with outstretched hands,
My heart parched and thirsty for your living water.

Fill my cup with your love, Lord.
Help me to feel your hands holding mine,
feel your arms around me,
feel your love empowering me.
Fill me with quietness and encouragement and trust.

Help me to live for you when trials, difficulties,
and storms hit me and those I love so deeply.
Help me not to give up when giving up seems easier.
Help me to trust you when I don't feel like
trusting anymore.

When I know pain, fill my cup with prayer.
Teach me the secrets of service and surrender.

Fill my cup, Lord. I lift it up to you.
Lift me up to do your will with love and sacrifice,
Never forgetting what you sacrificed for me—
Your Son.
My Messiah.
My Lord Jesus Christ.

Help me, Lord, to accept where I am now.
Help me to know I'm not stuck forever in my circumstances.
Help me remember that the windows do open
and that fresh breezes do blow in
and that living water forever flows
and that those who ask receive.

I'm asking now, Lord.
I'm holding my cup in my hands,
And I'm asking you to fill it . . . with you.
Fill my cup with
God the Father,
God the Son,
and God the Holy Spirit.

And when my cup springs a leak,
As earthen vessels are prone to do,
Then I'll just have to ask again,
Trusting in your love
To fill me again . . .
and thanking you!
Amen

Notes

1. *Beth Wohlford, "No Compromise," from Sunday bulletin of Willowcreek Community Church, 27 August 1995 p. 5.*

2. *C. W. Christian, "My Faith Is Small,"* Moonlight and Stuff *self-published, 1990. Used by permission.*